Murder at the Cellar

A FRESH START SMALL TOWN COZY MYSTERY

DANI SIMMS

TRILLIUM SAGE
PUBLISHING

Chapter One

I t had been a day just like any other when Avery found
the note. Well, that was a lie. It had been a tough day.
She had spent most of the day obsessing over every little
thing that had gone wrong in her life as she cleaned out the
first room of the dirty cellar. She'd always known that her
parents had gotten older, but when she discovered the rows
of cobweb-covered rooms in the second cellar, it became
apparent that they'd needed the help a lot sooner than they'd
gotten it. Not that she would ever have moved back to the
family vineyard if her husband hadn't died.

As she swept, she thought about every route her life had
already taken. She'd spent so much of her time on paths that
led her away from the vineyard, and, in the end, they all led
her back.

James would have loved this place, she thought as she
cleaned. She was right. It looked precisely like the perfect
setting for one of his crime novels. He would have hidden
something dangerous in every dark shadow that was there.

Although part of her missed the city, she was grateful to
be out of it. In her hometown, nobody knew James. It had

also been so long since she'd moved away that almost nobody knew Avery either. The benefit of that was that she wouldn't have to talk about it.

Shuffling her feet, she chased away the golden retriever puppy that threatened to disturb her dust pile. Her parents had insisted that she get a puppy. They said it would be good company, but all the puppy ever did was beg for attention and bark at stuff.

She'd decided to cut Sprinkles some slack, though. He was cute, and she liked knowing there was another living, breathing thing in the home with her.

Just as she thought she'd successfully chased the puppy away, she noticed something yellow in his mouth.

"Gimme that," she said, reaching for the dog.

It was pointless. He bounced and sprinted off into the deeper parts of the cellars. Avery chased after the pup, wondering if every statement regarding the trainability of a golden retriever had been a lie.

When she finally caught up with him, he seemed entirely uninterested in the item and let her take it back with grace.

"Please tell me I didn't just chase you all the way down here for a perfectly edible piece of paper," she huffed as she leaned against an old barrel.

The yellow paper was wet with gob as she turned it over in her hands. It was folded double, like the notes she used to pass around in school. Out of breath, she rested for a moment.

If it hadn't been for that one moment of rest, perhaps her stay at Le Blanc Cellars would have gone quite differently. Unfolding the paper, she held it at an angle in an attempt to get the best lighting.

*It is done. The owner of Le Blanc Cellars is gone, and we'll
never see his ugly face again. Don't worry; I cleaned up
properly. - F*

It read precisely like something her late husband would
have written in one of his crime novels. He would read them
to her, and she would help him piece together the stories
and clues. At that moment, she felt as if she could be one of
the leading ladies in one of his novels. Only, she wasn't some
busty blonde bombshell rummaging through the belongings of her rich boyfriend. She was covered in dust and
cobwebs, completely miserable, and had spent most of the
day scrubbing on her hands and knees.

She stared at the note for a while as she considered all
the different meanings it might have had. Who was the
owner of Le Blanc Cellars it was talking about? She'd grown
up on the vineyard, so she was certain that it wasn't her and
was almost certain it was none of her family. When the
sound of Sprinkles barking pulled her from her thoughts,
she tucked the note into her pocket and ran in his direction.
As usual, she found him barking toward the end room of
the cellars.

"Sprinkles!" she yelled through the dust. "Quit that! I've
told you, there's nothing there!"

Every puppy book she had read explained the obedient
nature of golden retrievers, but nothing she ever did could
stop Sprinkles from barking into the dusty darkness at the
end of the cellar rooms. Golden retrievers were supposed to
be easy to train, but she struggled with Sprinkles on a daily
basis. Avery figured perhaps he was as afraid of the dark as
she was.

She reached out to stroke the pup's head and caught a
glimpse of her watch.

"Oh no," she whispered.

Thanks to the insistence of her parents, she had agreed to attend the weekly Stammtisch at the neighboring vineyard. She hadn't known what that meant, so she looked it up. It seemed to be a reason for people with similar interests to get together and socialize. It wasn't exactly the kind of thing that Avery was into, but her parents had insisted.

The last thing she was in the mood for was to socialize with a group of women older than her, but she wouldn't mind a couple of glasses of wine. She figured she'd attend one, and then her parents would keep quiet about it.

With Sprinkles neatly tucked beneath her arm, she headed out of the cellar and rushed into the house to get ready.

Avery had been silent for most of the night, but the more she sipped her wine, the more she joined in on the conversation. She had to admit, as much as she hated it, that her mother had been right. The women of the Stammtisch were interesting and funny.

"So I believe you've just recently moved back?" asked Deb. "So what have you been keeping yourself busy with then?"

Deb was the youngest of the group. She'd married a wealthy vineyard owner and spent most of her time socializing. Avery had made a note to herself to remember that. She knew women like Deb often were the town gossip.

"Mostly spring cleaning," Avery joked. "You guys know how it goes."

The group mumbled an agreement in unison.

"So, have you found anything interesting yet?" Deb leaned into the table, eager to hear something she hadn't heard before.

Avery wasn't sure if it was the wine or the general desire to entertain Deb's need for information, but she reached into her back pocket and pulled out the note.

"Yeah, I found this note. If I didn't know any better, it might have something to do with Mr. Grier's death."

She handed the note around the table, and each woman took a turn to read it.

"Mr. Grier? That's the previous owner, isn't it?" Deb asked.

"Yes, he owned the property before my family took it over."

Deb's face scrunched slightly. "So what makes you think the note is about him?"

"Well, I don't know any other previous owners of the farm, so I just assumed."

The group laughed. "Yeah, but Mr. Grier isn't dead, is he?" Eleanor asked.

Eleanor was a plump, blonde woman. She'd been the one to start the Stammtisch after having spent some time in Germany.

"Yes, that's right," she continued, tapping her finger against her temples. "He disappeared as far as I can remember. Although I must admit, he would be the one they're referring to. I remember my parents talking about how unpleasant he was."

"Yes, that's right!" Camille piped in. "I remember them saying something like that. Very grumpy man. My brother said that he'd always found him rather creepy."

Camille was a freckle-faced scrawny woman who seemed to zone out only to rejoin the conversation when they were discussing something exciting. Avery was somewhat jealous of her ability to do that. Had she also been as capable of it, she might have saved herself from many painful conversations in the past.

"Yeah, you'll find no headstone with his name on it," Eleanor added. "It was the talk of the town. He just got fed up one day and left."

After that, the conversation quickly changed, and Avery sneaked outside for a breath of fresh air. It was the most socializing she had done in months, and she wasn't entirely sure she was doing all that well.

"I heard about your husband," Eleanor said from the doorway.

Avery had hoped to avoid the topic, but it seemed that conversations like that were unavoidable.

"Your mom told me," Eleanor eventually admitted.

"Ah."

Eleanor stepped out onto the patio and made herself comfortable next to Avery, who shuffled somewhat uncomfortably in place.

"I lost my husband a couple of years ago," she said with a kind smile. "I remember the months that followed and how quickly they turned into years. If I may, I'd like to offer you a small word of advice."

Avery didn't want to hear it, but she didn't want to be rude, either. So she forced a smile and nodded; at least Eleanor had the decency to ask. Most people just force-fed their unwanted advice.

"After my husband died, I found myself becoming consumed with every small this-and-that," she explained. "It was my attempt to fill a large space that he had left. The time we would normally have spent together, I spent obsessing over pointless things."

She handed Avery the folded-up note and shrugged. "Don't do that. In the end, it serves you no purpose. It only makes it nearly impossible to move on."

"Do you think you could move on now?" Avery asked.

"You mean re-marry?" she laughed. "Good Heavens, no,

but I can go out and do the things that interest me, and I can be comfortable with the quietness that is my home without him."

Avery tucked the note into her pocket. She appreciated Eleanor's advice, kind of, but she was in no way obsessing over anything. She was simply trying to survive an entirely new life without him.

Chapter Two

The next morning when Avery awoke, she was exhausted. For the third time that week, she'd had one too many sips of wine. She blinked as her eyes tried to focus on the brightness of the room. She hadn't even made it to bed.

She rolled off the couch and stumbled to the bathroom to get ready. Falling asleep on the couch was quickly becoming a regular occurrence for Avery. All the crime novels she'd helped James write and all the detective movies she'd watched when she was growing up had made it nearly impossible for her to sleep in total darkness.

Somehow, she felt less silly if she fell asleep in the well-lit lounge than she did going to sleep in her bedroom with a night light.

Dressed and with a strong cup of coffee placed firmly in her grip, she headed to the back door. Something stopped her in her tracks, though. On the table by the door, she saw the note she'd found sticking out from beneath the set of car keys that she'd carelessly tossed aside when she got home the previous night.

She couldn't keep her eyes off of it. The conversation from the night before was replaying in her head. Mr. Grier was missing, not dead, which made the note only more curious. Then immediately, she remembered Eleanor's words advising her not to become obsessed over small and pointless things.

Avery sighed as she lifted the car keys and the note and headed out the door to visit the local police station.

She was at the station for no more than two minutes before she was back in her car, the note still in hand. It seemed they found it as insignificant as everybody else had, and unless it was clearly stated that either a crime had been committed or there was foul play, it didn't mean anything. In other words, the note had been too vague for their liking. By the time she got back to the vineyard, she was ready to throw the note away and forget about it entirely.

But all that changed when she stepped into the wine room.

"Something on your mind?" Charles asked from behind the counter. "Did you not hear me greet you just then?"

"Sorry, Charles," she sighed. "Forgive me. I'm a little tired."

"So what are you reading then?" he asked with a cheeky smirk. "I used to be a cop, Avery. Nothing gets past me."

Avery looked at him for a moment as she decided whether it was even worth explaining the entire story to Charles, but his eyes kept glancing down at the note and something told her that he wasn't going to give up so easily.

Giving him the briefest summary of events, she handed him the note to inspect.

"And you tried to give this to the police?" he asked with a chuckle.

Avery nodded foolishly. "They said something about

how unlikely it is and something else I don't really remember. Anyway, they weren't very helpful."

Avery snatched the note back from Charles. A small part of her was afraid that he'd throw it away, and she'd only just found it. She wasn't sure why she was so reluctant to let it go. It just fit the description of the perfect clue so well.

Had James been there, he would have known that a note like that, in one of his books, was the most important clue of them all. Then it occurred to her that perhaps that's why she wouldn't throw it away. When she looked at it, she remembered how she would help James figure out the mysteries and storylines of his books. Something about that pointless piece of paper and the scribbles on it made her feel like he was still around.

"Yeah, well, that case is closed, so there'd be no reason to take on any new evidence," Charles said, but his eyes remained on the note in my hand.

"Well, thank you," Avery shrugged. She was only two steps away from him when he interrupted her thoughts again.

"It's an odd find, though," he said, reeling her back in. "You see, Mr. Grier's disappearance itself was odd."

Now he really had her curiosity. "In what way?"

"Well, for starters, it took weeks before anyone even noticed that he was gone. He wasn't the friendliest guy, you see, so nobody was really looking out for him."

"Yeah, I believe so," Avery chuckled.

"But eventually, they found the property abandoned. All he'd taken with him was one suitcase worth of clothing, and they only knew that because they had found the receipt for the suitcase on his dresser."

"So nobody went looking for him?" she asked.

"Why would they? Nobody knew anything about him, so they didn't even notice he was gone!" he laughed. "Eventually, though, when his debt piled up, the bank took the property from him and put it up for auction.”

It was only becoming more and more curious for Avery, and as her day progressed, she found herself reaching for the note more often. She read through the words over and over again as she tried to decipher precisely what it all could mean until, eventually, she decided it could only possibly mean exactly what it said, which wasn’t all that much.

That night though, when she tried to sleep, she found herself struggling to do so. Her mind was filled with thoughts of Mr. Grier. She’d never heard of someone being so unpleasant that an entire town wouldn’t notice they’d gone missing.

When she eventually fell asleep, it was with the light on.

⁓

A tall figure loomed at the doorway to the cellar. Avery immediately knew who it was. His face was contorted into a grumpy scowl, and his hair was slicked back with grease.

“What do you think you’re doing?” the man snapped at her. “Did I tell you it was alright for you to stop working?”

Avery stared at him in disbelief. She couldn’t remember the last time that anyone had spoken to her like that.

The man raised his hand and waved his bony finger in her direction.

“You’re no good for this farm. All you have to do is clean one measly cellar, and you can’t even seem to get that one right. I should have you sacked for this.”

“Mr. Grier?” she asked, her hands trembling slightly.

“Well, who else do you think it could be?” the man snarled, getting louder and louder the more frustrated he became. “This is my farm, isn’t it?”

Behind him, the door to the cellar swung open, and Avery could feel a cold air escape the space.

"Now get back there and keep cleaning like you're supposed to!" he ordered. "I won't ask you this nicely again."

When Avery's eyes flew open, she was drenched in sweat and grateful that she'd left the light on. Sprinkles had snuggled up close to her, and she was grateful for that too. She lay awake for hours afterward wondering why she would have such a vivid dream about a man she never knew and a man she never even cared about until just one day earlier.

As much as she tried to clear her mind and forget about the dream, it was no use. There was nothing else to distract her from it.

Avery reached for the notebook next to her bed and scribbled yet another item to her ever-growing to-do list.

"Buy television for the bedroom."

Chapter Three

Tired and unsettled, Avery stared at the entrance to the cellars. She'd cleared her day to keep cleaning, but she couldn't get herself to open the door and step inside. All she could see was the angry man from her dreams who had scolded her.

She rolled her head back and let out a loud sigh. She couldn't do it. So, she turned on her heels and headed for the path to the cottage that her parents were staying in. The sound of the gravel beneath her feet was familiar to her.

She had walked that path so many times as a child, but then she'd been too short to truly enjoy the view over the vines that grew in concentric rows on either side of her. Avery slowed her pace, looking out as far as she could see. It was certainly more peaceful than the city. She couldn't hear the traffic, trucks, or the neighbors.

The chill in the air kept her on her mission, though, and soon, she had reached the little cottage and knocked on the door.

"Who's there?" her mother called.

Avery rolled her eyes. "Are you kidding, Mom? Who else would it be?"

The door pulled open, and her mother smiled widely at her. "You never know when visitors might arrive unexpectedly."

It was something her mother had always said, yet there had hardly ever been a time when anyone would arrive unexpectedly at the house.

She stepped inside and peered around the home. There were items stacked upon each other as her parents tried to cram their belongings into the small cottage. They'd already gotten rid of a lot, and despite Avery mentioning that she'd be perfectly happy staying in the cottage, they'd insisted that she took the main house.

That meant, however, that their house was packed tight with items that they no longer had space for.

"I thought you were working in the cellars today," her mother commented as she reached for the pot of coffee.

"I don't know. I had a bad dream about it last night, so I thought I'd come to see what you are up to instead."

Avery hugged her dad, who greeted her cheerfully before taking a seat between two large heaps of pillows that occupied most of the sofa.

"Why on Earth would you dream about the cellar?" her father asked as a chuckle escaped him.

"I found a note down there that unsettled me," she answered with a shrug. "I suppose it snuck into my head as I slept."

"A note? What note?" her mother pressed.

Avery reached into her pocket and pulled out the now-crumpled piece of paper. She handed it to her mother, who read quickly through it before handing it to her father. After a few moments of searching for the glasses that had always remained neatly perched on his head, he trailed the words with his eyes.

"What does this mean?" he asked with a frown.

"I don't quite know," Avery answered. "But if you ask me, it certainly implies that something unpleasant came of Mr. Grier."

Her mother scoffed. "Oh please, Avery. You city folk are so used to crime and murder that you see it around every corner. There is no such thing here."

"You can't tell me I'm wrong about this," Avery argued. "This is exactly the kind of thing James would have used in one of his books. Read it again."

Her mother took the paper from her father's hand and read it again.

"This doesn't say anything about Mr. Grier on it…it only mentions an ugly owner," she joked, handing the paper back to Avery.

"I think our daughter's been under too much stress lately," her father said.

"Seriously, honey, why don't you take a break from the cellars and rest for the day?" her mother suggested.

"The only reason I have to be down there at all is because the two of you let it get into such bad condition!" Avery argued.

The rest of the conversation didn't go well. In fact, it felt similar to the lectures that she'd gone to during college. Her mother told her all about the newspaper article in which she read that bananas have an element responsible for curing depression. It was typical of her mother to turn the conversation to depression. Ever since Avery's aunt received a diagnosis of depression, her mother seemed to want to learn every available piece of information about it. The only problem was that her mother was elderly and gullible and would easily believe a single banana could cure depression.

With an arm-full of bananas, Avery left the cottage and headed home and curled up with a good book and a glass of wine. That glass of wine quickly turned into a few glasses of wine, and before she knew it, she was once again fast asleep on the couch.

There she remained in peace until the early hours of the morning when she awoke to the sound of Sprinkles barking non-stop. She rolled off the couch and peered through the window. Sprinkles seemed to be barking at nothing in particular, though he kept his eyes on the direction of the cellar door.

It gave Avery the chills, but she shook it off and strolled her way into the kitchen for a cup of tea. She considered going to quiet Sprinkles, but the thought of getting that close to the cellar while it was dark out felt like a bad idea, so she made herself comfortable again and put on a loud movie to drown out the noise.

Avery could feel the lack of sleep creeping in as she waited in the coffee shop for her childhood friend to join her. She looked around to see if she still recognized anybody there, but could only decide on one man, and even then, she couldn't be certain.

"Avery!" a voice called from the doorway.

Tiffany had been her best friend for all her childhood, but they hadn't seen each other much since Avery had moved away. She figured a catch-up session would be just the distraction she needed.

The women hugged and took their seats, and it felt to Avery as if no time had passed at all. It wasn't long before the women were talking freely.

"I believe you've been cleaning out the cellars," Tiffany said as she took a bite of cake.

"You've been speaking to my parents, I assume?" Avery joked. "Did they tell you about the note too?"

Avery had meant it as a joke, but it certainly caught Tiffany's attention.

"What note?" she asked with a curious frown.

Avery handed her the note to read. Tiffany read it a few times before nodding and handing it back.

"I see," she said. "And you think there's something there?"

"Don't you?" Avery teased.

"Do you remember when we were kids? You would watch all those crime movies and series and stuff," Tiffany said. "You'd watch all those detective shows, and then for weeks afterward, you'd have me running around chasing imaginary clues."

"Oh, c'mon," Avery argued. "It can't have been that bad!"

Tiffany nodded enthusiastically. "Yeah. Don't you remember that one time you had us all convinced that our chemistry teacher was smuggling drugs? You even had a group of us stake out his house one night. We all got the flu! It was terrible!"

Avery had almost forgotten about that night. They'd all gotten into so much trouble. Four of them had snuck out of the house intending to catch their teacher in the act. It had backfired, though. They discovered nothing and wound up bedridden for days.

"Do you think I'm making too much of this note, then?" Avery asked.

"I mean, it doesn't really say all that much, does it?" Tiffany said. "Besides, as far as I believe, the previous owner never died. He just packed up and left."

"So I've been told," Avery answered. "But don't you think that's strange?"

"I suppose," Tiffany answered with a shrug. "He was kind of a weird guy, though. It's not strange when weird men do weird things."

Tiffany's answer made Avery laugh. It had been such a typical thing for her to say. As they continued their conversation, Avery thought about the note and what Tiffany had said. She thought perhaps she was making a fuss where no fuss was required.

One thing was for certain. Everyone seemed to agree with the police about it. They all felt that there was nothing to it and that the note was of no importance at all.

With the opinion of the entire world against her, she decided to abandon the notion that the note had anything to do with Mr. Grier's disappearance and did her best to bury it in her mind.

Chapter Four

The next day, Avery wasted no time getting back into cleaning out the cellar. Her coffee with Tiffany reminded her that she'd always made a big deal out of things that were unimportant. So, she forgot about the note and carried on with the task at hand.

The music was on, the weather was pleasant, and Avery was in a good mood. She hadn't been in such a good mood in weeks, and so she figured she'd make the most of it. She danced around as she swept, clearing cobwebs and dust from every corner.

She hadn't yet decided what to do with the cellar once she'd gotten it clean, but she knew she could use the space for something. One thing was for certain, though. With the dark rooms and shadowy corners, she'd be transforming that place into an annual Halloween attraction.

Every now and then, she'd find small items that someone had left behind in the cellar. Some of them she put aside, hoping to get a better look at them later, but most of them wound up on the trash heap.

She moved into the next small room, taking a look

around at the amount of work that she had ahead of her. It was by far the dustiest room she'd been in yet. Cobwebs hung from the ceiling so low that she was worried she'd breathe them in.

With no time to waste, she got to work. She was making good progress until she took a step backward and found herself on unstable ground. The floorboards beneath her were so old and weakened that they completely gave way and her foot went right through the floor.

Off balance, she fell backward as the edges of the wood scraped her ankle. She cursed her parents as she rolled on the ground, cradling her aching foot. She blamed them for her injury, considering they were the ones who'd let the cellars get into such bad condition in the first place.

Avery rolled on her side to inspect the damage to the floor. Although the hole she'd left behind wasn't too big, it was apparent that a large section of the floor was too soft to step on. She could see that some of the wood had been cut, removed, and then placed back.

Usually, that would have meant that someone had replaced the floor. But the grain on these planks of wood still lined up. It made no sense to her.

Avery got onto her feet and limped closer to the hole she'd created. That's when she noticed a handle sticking out from behind one of the broken pieces of wood. She reached carefully into the hole, afraid of what creepy crawlies might come jumping out at her.

With her fingers wrapped tightly around the handle, she tugged. Whatever it was, it was fairly secured in place and needed a hard tug before it finally released. Avery had put all her energy into that final tug, and with her aching ankle, she fell backward again.

"Damn it!" she yelled, coughing up a cloud of dust.

She pulled the item closer to her to inspect it and found

that it was an old suitcase. The idea of a suitcase underneath the floorboards immediately piqued her curiosity. She'd never heard of that being a place to store such a thing and assumed that there had to be something valuable inside.

She pressed her thumbs against the latches of the suitcase, and they unclipped easily. She braced herself for what treasures she might find and pulled the lid open.

All she found were some dusty clothes and a pair of men's shoes. In the corner, she saw a box that seemed to be an older shaving kit of some kind.

"Who keeps clothes underneath the floorboards?" she asked herself.

She was about to remove the clothes, to check if perhaps something more interesting was hidden underneath when she spotted the name inscribed on the lining of the suitcase: George R. Grier.

A pit formed in her stomach as she realized that the suitcase of clothing belonged to the previous owner. The very man who'd scolded her in her dreams to keep cleaning the cellars. She stared at the suitcase, desperately trying to understand its significance.

Then she remembered her conversation with Charles. He had mentioned that Mr. Grier had disappeared with nothing but a suitcase of clothing. Immediately she wondered if she had found that missing suitcase.

Nervously, she slammed the lid closed and pinched her eyes shut.

"It's nothing," she whispered to herself. "It's just a coincidence. These things happen every day."

Then she sighed. "No, they don't," she mumbled. "People don't find suitcases hidden under floorboards every day."

She inspected the outside of the suitcase for anything else that could possibly explain why it was tucked away in its hiding place. She saw nothing but a few dried up drops of a dark liquid.

For a moment, she thought it could be blood. Then, she remembered she had no idea what dried blood was supposed to look like, and it could be anything. She recalled once, when researching for one of her husband's books, she'd learned that rust could sometimes have a similar color to dried blood.

"It could just be rust," she said to herself in a feeble attempt to calm herself down. Somewhere in the depths of her mind, she knew it wasn't rust, no matter how much she wished it was. She wanted it to be anything other than blood.

The longer she stared at the case, the colder she felt. The hairs on the back of her neck began to rise. So she grabbed the case by the handle and headed for the door as fast as she could. She didn't know what she would do with it, but she knew that she wanted to get out of the cellar and fast.

With the suitcase perched neatly on her coffee table, she paced. Her conversation with Charles about how Mr. Grier had died replayed in her head over and over again as she tried to figure out if she'd missed some or other details.

Go to the police, she thought.

No, she'd already tried that, and they had turned her away. They seemed entirely uninterested in the case. She then considered hunting for any possible contact details for Mr. Grier. But he had disappeared. If anyone had details for him, the bank would never have taken his property from him.

Her mind was swimming with the possibilities. Had the case accidentally wound up beneath the floor? No, that seemed unlikely. Could the case belong to a different Mr. Grier? That was possible.

Eager to put her mind at ease, she dialed the number to her parent's cottage.

"Hi, Mom, it's me," she said as soon as she heard someone had answered the call.

"What's up, honey?" her mother's kind voice responded.

"Mom, do you remember the name of the Mr. Grier that owned the vineyard before us?"

"You're not still wondering about that note, are you?" her mother replied, a hint of frustration in her voice.

"No, this is something else," Avery responded impatiently. "Now, do you remember?"

"Hang on, let me ask your father."

Avery paced as she listened to the muffled conversation in the background. Usually, having to wait like that would frustrate her, but she didn't mind the wait. The longer she waited, the more she could believe that the suitcase merely belonged to someone else.

"Hi, honey," her mother answered. "Your father says he doesn't remember the entire name, but he remembers that the middle name was Reuben.

It added up. Avery swallowed hard and did her best not to sound nervous.

"Was his first name George?" she asked.

"Yes! George! That's it," her mother cheered. "But if you already knew that, why on Earth are you asking me?"

"What? No," Avery said. "I found something with a name on it, and I was wondering if it had perhaps belonged to him."

"Oh, okay. Well, if you were hoping to return it to him, I'd give up on that now already. Nobody's seen or heard from him since he left the farm."

Avery ended the call with her mother and collapsed onto the couch. She had hoped that her mother would give her a different name. She had hoped that the case belonged to someone else. But it didn't. It belonged to him.

With the note and the case combined, she could no longer ignore it. She had stumbled across something that should never have been found, and she had no idea what to do with any of it. She knew her parents wouldn't be of any help.

So, she reached for her phone and opened the Stammtisch group chat.

> *Hi ladies.*
>
> *I need your help. I've found the missing suitcase in the Mr. Grier case. Can you all come to my house this evening and tell me I'm not nuts?*

With that, she attached the photograph of the suitcase and waited.

Chapter Five

A few hours after she'd messaged them, the women of the Stammtisch filled Avery's home. It seemed that in a small town, even the smallest drop of drama was enough to fill each woman's cup. It was less about solving a crime and more about having something new to talk about. The rest of what they did was just added fun. Everyone sipped merrily on a glass of wine except Avery. She was too stressed to stomach any alcohol that day. She stuck to a warm cup of tea.

Deb had suggested that they create what she called a murder map where they could put all the evidence and ideas against the wall and connect the dots with red string. She'd even brought the red string along with her.

Despite Avery feeling fearful about it all, the rest of the women seemed excited. They looked like something out of a low-budget crime series. The living room was scattered with small bits of paper and string.

"Okay, okay," said Deb, waving her glass of wine through the air. "Let's take a look at our suspects and reenact how they might have done it. That way, we can spot anything we might have missed."

"Let's start with the chief of police," said Eleanor.

The very tired Avery couldn't even remember how they had decided that the chief of police would be a suspect, but his name was up on the wall. The scene that occurred before her was nothing short of ridiculous. Eleanor frowned and put on her deepest voice as she pretended to be the police chief. Deb, who was acting as Mr. Grier, stood on her toes to make herself taller.

When Eleanor, the police chief, confronted Deb, Mr. Grier, about his antisocial behavior the group burst out laughing and could no longer continue with the exercise.

When the laughter eventually died down, Eleanor frowned again and scanned the room.

"Where's Nobbie?" she asked.

Avery had almost forgotten that Eleanor had brought her German shepherd along for the exercise. The group hopped up and searched the room.

"I think Nobbie and Sprinkles were chasing after something the last time I saw them," Deb piped up.

Eleanor's eyes stretched wide, and she ran for the back door.

"He better not be eating anything he shouldn't!" she panicked. "He's got the weakest stomach on the planet!"

By the time the four women made it out the back door, Nobbie was already ill. Avery thought for a moment that he physically looked green but realized soon that it was likely the lack of decent sleep.

"Nobbie! What have you eaten?" Eleanor shouted as she ran towards the dog.

The women watched as Eleanor felt Nobbie's ears and throat. She even managed to pry open his mouth and have a look inside.

"I need to get him to the vet; you lot carry on without me," she said.

Then, with strength that seemingly came out of nowhere, she lifted the large dog into her arms and started walking toward her car.

"You're not going without me!" Deb called, running inside to get her bag and keys.

Avery and Camille decided they weren't going to stay behind on their own either. So, the four women piled into Avery's car and raced off to the vet. Poor Nobbie lay sprawled out over the legs of Eleanor and Deb, who had drawn the short straw and sat uncomfortably on the back seat.

Despite the new vet in town being busy when they got there, Eleanor wangled her way ahead of everybody and into his treatment room. She hadn't even bothered to close the door.

"Nobbie's eaten something, and he's ill, and I won't leave here until you fix him," she demanded.

She really seemed to be quite panicked about it, but Avery could understand. The one thing she and Eleanor had in common was that both their husbands had died. Nobbie was her only companion.

"I've been thinking, Avery," Deb said as they paced the waiting room. "How do we know the suitcase even has anything to do with anything?"

Avery sighed. "I guess we don't. Would you take the fact that I have a gut feeling as the answer?"

Deb thought about it for a moment and nodded. "So then, if this were one of your husband's books, what would they do next?"

A pit formed in Avery's stomach as she processed the question. She wished she could just ask him. She wished that all of it was just part of another one of his books. But he wasn't there anymore, and still, she knew the answer.

"I suppose the character would figure out what those red droplets are on the lid of the suitcase."

At that moment, Camille came to nudge them in the ribs and pointed in the direction of the treatment room.

"Do you guys see what I see?" she asked.

The vet was treating the dog, but every few seconds, he would look up and admire another part of Eleanor's body. Every few seconds, he needed to tell her what he'd discovered with whatever test he was doing, and a slight rosiness flushed across his cheeks.

"Looks like Eleanor's got herself an admirer," Deb whispered.

Avery chuckled. The vet was handsome, but Eleanor had made it clear to her that she was in no way ready to move on, and she wondered how Eleanor would handle the situation. That was, of course, if the vet had the guts to even pull a move on her. He'd briefly explained earlier that he'd also moved from the city. It was likely that he felt as out of place as Avery did. So it was unlikely that he'd make a move on Eleanor any time soon. But it wasn't going to stop him from staring.

Eleanor hadn't noticed at all. She clung to Nobbie as if she'd never see him again. When the vet handed her a tablet and explained that the dog would be right as rain by the morning, Eleanor threw her arms around him and thanked him.

The vet blushed even brighter, closing his eyes to enjoy the embrace. Of course, the three women in the waiting room burst into laughter. There was no such thing as subtlety after that many glasses of wine.

They cheered as Eleanor led Nobbie back into the waiting room.

"He's going to be fine thanks to..." her voice trailed off as she realized she hadn't even bothered to ask the vet what his name was.

"Oh, uh...Dr. Moses," he replied sheepishly. "Samuel Moses."

"Samuel Moses?" Eleanor asked with surprise. "How absolutely Biblical! Anyway, thank you again."

Dr. Moses watched Eleanor closely as she settled the bill. He'd given her a massive discount, but Avery was sure that if it were allowed, he would have given her a total discount. He really couldn't help but gawk at her.

Just as they were about to leave, they heard him pipe up from behind them.

"You know..." he said. "I couldn't help but overhear you earlier. You said something about a suitcase?"

Avery would have preferred if they didn't have to tell him, but Deb didn't seem bothered to share any information.

"Oh, yes!" she exclaimed. "It's all very exciting. We think it might have blood on it. We were just saying that we should get it tested."

"It might not be my place, but I could do some tests," he offered, glancing over at Eleanor. "I—I mean, I wouldn't be able to tell you whose blood it is, or if it is human or animal blood...but I can tell you if it is blood at all."

Deb gasped with excitement. "That would be so helpful! Thank you!" she cheered.

Avery was sure that he was only offering a feeble attempt to impress Eleanor, but she was certainly going to take him up on the offer.

"That would be great!" she said. "I could bring it to you in the morning?"

Dr. Moses perked up with excitement as he glanced back over at Eleanor, but she only had eyes for Nobbie.

"Yes, of course," he agreed.

The next morning, with a little more rest, she seriously regretted taking Dr. Moses up on his offer. She didn't want to look further into the matter, but she'd agreed to meet him twenty minutes before his practice opened, and she'd over-slept. So, there was no more time to cancel.

She pulled up at the veterinary practice, and Dr. Moses eagerly awaited her. When she climbed out of the car with nothing but the suitcase in hand, she couldn't help but notice his eyes watching to see if anyone had come with her. She was sure he was looking for Eleanor.

"Oh, uh, good morning um..." he said, holding his hand out for Avery.

"Avery," she said with a smile as she shook his hand. "Good morning, Samuel Moses. Thank you so much for helping us."

"It's no problem at all," he said with a dazzling smile. "Come on in."

There was an awkward silence as she watched him scrape some of the liquid off the lid. He seemed disappointed that she had come alone, and she wasn't entirely sure what they could talk about while they waited.

Thankfully, he disappeared into a back room for a few minutes and Avery could rest her head back on the wall. When he returned, he had a puzzled look on his face.

"That can't be good," Avery said sarcastically as he approached.

"Well Avery, I can't tell you much more, but I can tell you that the liquid is definitely blood."

Chapter Six

A very dropped the suitcase right by her front door as she got back home. She couldn't look at it any longer; it gave her the creeps. She needed a distraction from it all. Whenever she thought she could forget it and ignore it, the situation only got more bizarre.

Some part of her thought perhaps it was James doing this, that maybe his spirit had created this elaborate game for her to keep her busy enough to forget about how depressing her life had become. But that also seemed absurd. It all seemed absurd to her, and yet she could not ignore it.

Avery knew what she needed to do. It was the only thing that had ever given her comfort when times got hard, other than James. And he wasn't there, so she had to stick to the only remaining option. Avery hurried to the kitchen to prepare her favorite breakfast of Souffle Toast. She would fill the pit in her stomach with the fluffy goodness of the eggy souffle-like French toast and fresh berries. Ordinarily, Avery would have loved to enjoy her breakfast with a refreshing mimosa, but there was too much work to be done today, so she settled for a cinnamon latte. She made a mental note: mimosas next time.

The food had done the trick. In fact, it had done more than that. It had not only distracted her but it had cheered her up enough to the point where she was humming a happy tune to herself as she did the dishes.

She figured she couldn't spend another entire day not being productive, and she wasn't quite ready to face the cellars yet. So, she headed to the wine room to see what Charles was doing.

"Morning, Charles," she sang as she entered.

The tasting room was impressive. Beautifully kept barrels and crystal chandeliers filled the room. Every window had a view of the vineyard, and soft jazz was playing at all times. Charles stood behind a large circular counter that filled the center of the space, ready to serve any wine tasters that might enter.

"Good morning, Avery," he greeted. "You're chipper this morning."

"Good food will do that to you, Charles," Avery teased. "How are things here?"

"Same old, same old," he answered. "Although I must admit, since you've come back to the farm, I'm seeing a lot of the locals come by. I guess they're coming to see if you've made any changes."

"Should I?"

Avery had never planned on running the vineyard, so she didn't exactly have a plan in place. She knew some areas needed cleaning and rejuvenation, but she had never considered that perhaps everything had become outdated.

"I like it just the way it is," Charles said. "Oh, before I forget," he continued, "a letter came for you."

Charles held out a brown envelope with the words "To

the lady of Le Blanc Cellars" scribbled on it in bad hand-writing.

"Who on Earth would be sending me letters?" Avery asked, snatching it from him.

"Beats me," Charles said. "The postman delivered it."

"Tell me, Charles," Avery said. "You're still pretty young-ish. Too young for retirement, at least. Why did you stop being a cop?"

Charles sighed and leaned against the wooden counter. "Honestly?" he said. "It was all the paperwork. My hand started to cramp!"

Avery took a moment before she realized he was joking. She had only half been listening anyway, she couldn't stop thinking about the note and who it would be from.

"Just kidding," he laughed. "I guess being a policeman wasn't all I thought it would be, and after many years, I yearned for something a little more peaceful."

Charles motioned to his surroundings as he spoke. He had always taken great pride in the work that he'd done in the wine room. He treated it like his own little kingdom, and it showed.

Avery didn't say a word. Her mind thought only about the letter as she trailed her fingers across the words on the envelope.

"Open it," Charles sighed.

"I'm sorry, Charles." Avery's shoulders dropped. "I was listening, I promise. It's just...this is so strange."

"Come now," he teased. "I'm just as curious as you are about it. Maybe it's from a secret admirer."

"Oh goodness, I hope not," Avery said as her eyes widened.

For a moment, she thought she saw Charles drop his shoulders as if her comment had disappointed him somehow, but she thought nothing of it and ripped the envelope open.

Stop poking your nose where it doesn't belong. Sometimes you should just leave things where you've found them.

Let it go or suffer the consequences.

Avery felt her knees go weak as her hands began to tremble. When the color drained from her face, Charles snatched the letter and scanned through it.

"What is this supposed to mean?" he asked, waving the letter.

"The stuff..." she muttered. "From the cellars. I think it has to do with that and the blood and..."

Avery had to sit down; she could feel herself getting dizzy.

"The blood?" Charles was pouring her a glass of ice water.

"Yes," she answered. "The vet tested the blood...on the suitcase. He says it's blood."

She was no longer making perfect sense. Charles looked at her with great concern. She saw the letter on the counter in front of her and reached out for it again. She read it again, hoping that this time by some miracle it would say something else.

It didn't. She read the same words over and over.

"Go to the police," Charles urged her.

"I've been there. They won't believe me!"

"They will know that you've got the letter," he answered. "Avery, whoever it is, they're threatening you, and the police should know about it."

She took a moment to think it over. In her mind, she

had visions of someone busting down her door and burying her under the floorboards, just as they had hidden away the suitcase.

"Okay," she finally agreed.

She reached out to take the letter, but her hands were trembling too much, and she lost her grip. The letter floated down to the ground. No sooner had it made contact with the floor, and Sprinkles had it in his grip, and he bolted out the door.

"Sprinkles! No!" Avery shouted as she chased after the dog.

It was no use. Sprinkles was halfway across the lawn by the time Avery had made it out of the door. Small bits of brown paper scattered across the green grass like confetti. It was her best piece of evidence, and it had become completely useless.

"Well, that won't work," Charles said, being of no help at all. "Just...take care of yourself, Avery."

Charles raised his hand as if he was going to pat her on the back but seemed to change his mind last minute. Instead, he balled his hand into a fist and retreated into the wine room.

Avery collected what bits of paper she could find and headed back home. She laid them out on the coffee table, trying desperately to piece the letter together, but Sprinkles had swallowed some of it, and most of what she had couldn't be put into any kind of order. The best she could get was the word "nose," and that meant absolutely nothing.

She spent the next few hours pacing in her living room, agonizing over the letter. Who could it be from? What did it have to do with the suitcase and the note? How did they know?

Avery's mind was swimming with questions that she didn't have the answers to. It made no sense to her. She had somehow survived most of her life in the city without finding herself in the middle of the drama. She'd hardly been back in her hometown, and she was already making a reputation for herself.

She stared out of the window towards her parent's cottage as she tried to decide whether or not she should tell them about it. Avery wasn't sure she could speak to anyone now. She barely knew anybody there, and still, somehow, someone knew about the items she had found.

Again, she reached for her phone and opened up the Stammtisch group chat.

Somebody knows about the items. I've been threatened. I know how this sounds. I promise I'm not crazy. Come by tomorrow, and I'll tell you all about it.

Avery collapsed onto the couch. She knew that there was no way she would get any sleep that night. She was too afraid. She considered for a moment asking Charles if he would stay in the house with her, but something about his body language earlier made her think perhaps he would feel uncomfortable with it. She was, after all, his boss.

Instead, she closed all the curtains, switched on all the lights, made herself a strong pot of coffee, and put on a movie. Sprinkles was placed on the couch beside her, and she wouldn't let him leave until she was certain that the sun had risen and that she had made it safely through the night.

Chapter Seven

Avery's driveway was full of cars, and dishes were sprawled all through Avery's home as everybody wrapped up their lunch. It wasn't just the women of the Stammtisch that had arrived; they'd brought along Tiffany and Dr. Moses too. Avery thought the addition of the vet was strange, but according to Eleanor, he'd taken great interest in it all, and she insisted he could be of assistance.

He had already become involved when he concluded that the substance on the suitcase had been blood, so Avery agreed to let him tag along. Besides, she got a kick out of watching him do his best to get Eleanor's attention. Unfortunately for him, she seemed entirely uninterested and oblivious.

The group passed around the torn pieces of the letter, asking Avery to repeat the full message over and over as they analyzed it. Eventually, Eleanor slumped back on the couch and sighed, nearly spilling half her glass of red wine all over herself.

"I just don't understand," she mumbled. "How would they even know about all of this?"

Without missing a beat, Camille looked in Deb's direction. The room fell silent as Deb attempted to pretend that she hadn't noticed everybody looking at her. It only took a few seconds before she dropped her shoulders.

"Okay, I have to admit to something," she said, breaking the silence. "I might have told a couple of people around town about our little crime investigation thingy."

"You can't help yourself, can you?" Camille complained, waving her palms to the sky.

"I just thought that maybe if I told a few people, they might know something and might be able to help!" she argued.

"Well, look what's happened. Now, poor Avery here is receiving death threats," Camille countered.

"Death threats?" Avery piped up. "It didn't say anything about death there."

"Suffer the consequences," Eleanor chimed in. "That sounds an awful lot like a death threat to me."

"I suppose it doesn't matter," Dr. Moses added. "What matters is Avery received the letter, and we need to figure out who it was."

A smug grin broke across Deb's face. "I agree with Sam here, so let's brainstorm this a little."

"Alright," Avery said, clasping her hands together. "Deb, who exactly did you tell about this?"

"Not too many people," Deb sighed. "Mrs. Greene at the bakery, the hairdresser, the lady who sells the perfumes down at the center, and I think maybe a couple of family members?"

Avery pressed her fingers to her temples. "And I suppose all those people could have told a whole bunch of people, so this really doesn't narrow it down, does it?"

"I'm afraid not," Dr. Moses said as he slumped back in his chair.

"And I think we're going to need some more wine," Eleanor added.

Dr. Moses didn't hesitate to fill her glass while Avery went to fetch another few bottles. The more they drank, the more elaborate their schemes became on how they could catch whoever wrote the note.

"I know!" Camille chimed. "Why don't we ask our little gossip, Deb, to tell everyone that Avery had taken the belongings and buried them somewhere in a field or something...then, we wait to see who comes looking for them."

There was a short silence as the group thought it through. For a moment it, seemed like a good idea, but hope quickly faded.

"How long do you think we'd have to stake out the field then?" Dr. Moses asked.

There was an exasperated sigh through the group as they realized that yet another great idea was, in fact, a rather terrible idea.

Hours later, with no conclusion, Avery found herself alone at home again. They'd all had too much to drink, and Dr. Moses had even had to take Eleanor home, so her car still sat in the driveway. Despite all the wine, there was no way that Avery could sleep.

She was too terrified to close her eyes, afraid that with the amount of alcohol she'd consumed, she wouldn't hear if someone had broken into her house to make her "suffer the consequences."

On the television, she watched reruns of all her favorite shows, but when those made her too sleepy, she picked out the worst action movie she could find and turned the volume to full. On her couch, she perched for the night, eager to see the sunrise in the morning.

Charles hadn't seen Avery for two days, and when she walked into the wine room that morning, it was clear to him that she hadn't slept since. Dark rings hung underneath her usually sparkling eyes.

She looked dull that day, a word he never thought could ever describe her. She had lost her cheerful smile and warm greeting.

"How's it going, Charles," she said through yawns as she planted herself on a seat at his counter.

"Forgive my forwardness," he answered, "but you look terrible. When's the last time you slept?"

"I dunno," she shrugged. "When did I get that letter?"

Charles placed his hands flat on the counter and leaned forward. "I saw some cars outside when I left yesterday. It looked like you were having a party."

"We got together," she yawned again. "To see what we could do to identify who wrote the note since I'm pretty certain the police won't help me."

"Well," Charles smiled, handing her a glass of water. "I might not be police anymore...but I've got a plan."

Avery slowly lowered the glass from her lips and frowned at him. "Really?"

He reached under the table and pulled out a guest book and a pen.

"Remember when I told you that we've been getting a lot of locals here lately?" he asked. "Well, I figured that at some point, this mystery man...or woman would probably come by to scout things out."

"Okay," Avery said. She followed but not entirely.

"So, I thought I'd ask them all to write in the guest list," he said proudly. "Then we could compare the handwriting to see if there's a match."

It was a good idea. In fact, to Avery, it was a genius idea.

It was certainly the only idea she'd heard so far that would actually work.

"Yes," she agreed. "That could definitely work. Very clever, Charles."

"I suppose not clever enough for a raise?" he joked.

"No, but if it works, I might just kiss you," she teased.

Charles cleared his throat and looked away quickly. It had slipped out, and Avery hadn't meant it.

"I'm sorry, Charles, I'm just tired," she said. "I didn't mean to be so inappropriate."

"Don't worry about it, Avery," he smiled. "But how about you get some rest...and a shower, perhaps?"

Avery happily agreed. She'd caught a glimpse of herself in the mirror before she left, and she knew it wasn't a pretty sight. She needed to leave before the customers arrived, or she might have scared them off.

"Thanks, Charles," she said kindly.

Charles winked at her. "Anything for you, boss."

Chapter Eight

Avery had been sitting and staring for hours. Her mind swam with too many various possibilities, and she could feel her sanity slowly slipping away from her. So, she decided to distract herself with a trip to town.

The town wasn't big, and she'd seen most of the shops so often that she could tell you what you'd find on each shelf. It did help as a distraction, though.

As usual, her first stop was the coffee shop. She was eager for something bitter but also sweet. She paid little attention as she pushed past the tables and chairs and toward the counter to place her order.

When she had her coffee in hand and was headed back toward the street, she was stopped by a familiar voice.

"Avery!" Eleanor said, flustered.

Avery looked at her. She was seated rather closely to Dr. Moses. They both seemed a little embarrassed and had obviously assumed she'd spotted them. In reality, Avery had been so distracted that day that, had they not called her name, she wouldn't have noticed.

"Hey guys," Avery greeted cheerfully. "What are you guys up to?"

Eleanor's cheeks turned bright pink. "Oh, you know, we're just getting a cup of coffee and such."

It was a bizarre answer, but Avery figured she wouldn't press any further. Quite clearly, the two were on a date and weren't expecting to be found out. And Avery didn't have the energy to get into details.

"Great!" Avery answered. "I'm just doing a bit of window shopping in this good weather."

Eleanor and Dr. Moses glanced outside, where dark clouds were rolling in, threatening a more-than-imminent storm. Then, they glanced at each other awkwardly.

"Well, let me know if you spot anything good," Eleanor said with a sweet smile.

"Sure!"

Avery turned to leave, but Dr. Moses reached out a hand and tapped her lightly on the elbow.

"Um, Avery, just a second," he said gently. "I've actually got something for you."

He reached into his briefcase and pulled out a sealed envelope. He handed it over to a very puzzled Avery.

"I have a friend in the city," he explained. "He works in some lab where they do DNA testing and stuff. It's all very complicated, and I never know what he's rattling on about."

"Okay?" Avery said, sounding more annoyed than she'd liked.

"Well, he owed me a big favor. I once did surgery for him for free...anyway, I called in the favor and sent over the small amount of that blood I gathered. He said he'd test it to see if it matches anybody on their national system."

Avery gripped the envelope tight. "And?"

"Well," he gestures to the envelope. "I haven't opened it

yet. Figured it was something that you should do first. Keep in mind it might not have any answers at all."

"Thank you for doing this," she said with a smile. "It means a lot."

He nodded. "If I may ask, though," he continued, "I am rather curious. Would you mind opening it now? I've been wondering all week what it might say."

Avery swallowed hard and nodded. She wasn't sure if she was ready to know the answers yet. She had planned on leaving it on her mantle for at least a week before she found the courage to open it.

But Dr. Moses seemed so excited, and Eleanor had already leaned in to listen.

Nervously, Avery peeled open the envelope and pulled out the paper. Most of it had information on it she didn't understand. Then, at the bottom, she saw one final piece of information.

"The..." she was struggling to speak, and her hands had started to shake. "The blood is a match to Mr. G.R. Grier."

There was a gasp from both Eleanor and Dr. Moses.

"You were right!" Eleanor whispered, looking around to make sure that nobody had heard her.

Avery couldn't believe the information, and she had no idea what to do with it either. She wasn't even home yet, and she had decided she didn't want to be there alone. She had been right, meaning that the threat in the letter she'd received could be very real.

By the time she got home, Tiffany was already waiting for her. She'd invited her over for lunch, hoping to continue to distract herself from her increasing levels of stress.

"Sorry I made you wait," she said, clambering out of the car.

"It's no problem," Tiffany laughed. "I'm fashionably early, as usual."

"You choose the wine, and I'll get started on the food," Avery said, ushering Tiffany inside.

"What are you making for lunch?" Tiffany hollered while looking through the wine fridge.

"I've got this yummy couscous and shrimp dish I've been wanting to make for you," Avery called back from the kitchen.

Tiffany reached into the fridge and pulled out the newest release from Le Blanc Cellars. "Ooh…shrimp. Perfect! I've heard so much about your new rosé, and this should pair very nicely with shrimp," Tiffany said as she began rummaging through a drawer for a corkscrew.

Over lunch, Avery had agonized over every detail of the case. Tiffany was only growing more concerned about her friend and wasn't certain what to do about it. It was clear to her that no matter how hard Avery tried, she couldn't keep her mind off it.

"Then there's the blood," Avery said, taking a large bite of food. The varied textures and tastes of the couscous, shrimp, and asparagus mixture made her taste buds sing. Tiffany had done a fine job selecting the wine to match their lunch.

"Yes, that vet guy said it was human, but it could be anybody's, Avery. Someone could have cut themselves in the cellar, and it could have dripped between the floorboards and splashed all over the suitcase."

Avery shook her head, turning pale. "No," she said. "That vet guy had it sent to some special lab."

"Had what sent?"

"The blood! Keep up, will you, Tiff?" Avery joked.

"Did they get back to him?" Tiffany asked as her eyes widened, and she leaned in closer.

"Yes," Avery cried, throwing her hands in the air. "It's a match to Mr. Grier!"

"Oh, my," Tiffany said, her eyes drifting off as she thought it all over. "Well, it was his clothing, so surely there could be blood? I mean, there could be a million reasons for his blood to be on there. Maybe he had nosebleeds."

"You don't send death threats for the discovery of a nosebleed," Avery said dryly.

"Oh, come now, that letter was nothing more than a nasty prank."

"C'mon, Tiff," Avery said. "You have to agree that it's odd to bury a suitcase with clothes in it underneath the floorboards of the cellar, right? Blood or no blood, that's a pretty weird thing to do."

Tiffany took a sip of her wine and thought it over.

"I suppose you're right," she said.

The two women sat in silence as they finished their meal. Each of them was contemplating all the various realities of what might have happened down in that cellar. Soon, the sun had set, and the farm was dark.

Tiffany was helping Avery clean up when the sound of barking startled them both, sending a plate crashing to the ground.

"Sprinkles!" Avery called, opening the door for the puppy.

But he just kept barking.

"Sprinkles! Get in here!" she called but got no response.

"What is he even barking at?" Tiffany asked. "Shouldn't we go check?"

Avery sighed. "I bet you ten bucks he's barking at that cellar door. He's been doing it for weeks now."

Tiffany accepted the bet, and the two women made their

way across the lawn toward the cellar. As expected, they found Sprinkles. His nose was pressed to the crack of the door as he growled loudly.

"Do you think there could be mice or bats or something?" Tiffany asked, shining a flashlight towards the door.

"More like the ghost of Mr. Grier," Avery answered as she clipped the lead to Sprinkles' collar.

Tiffany sighed. "Avery, you can't keep doing this. I beg of you, take everything you have to the police."

Chapter Nine

Avery was more frustrated than she would have liked to admit, and Tiffany's suggestion of going to the police irritated her. Surely, Tiffany didn't think she was dumb enough not to have gone to the authorities.

"Don't you think I've tried that?" Avery argued. "They turned me away. They said that I had no proof of where I found the items and no proof that anything sinister had happened."

"What about the letter? Surely they'll take that seriously?" Tiffany asked.

Avery let out a loud sigh and rolled her eyes.

"There's hardly anything left of it. It could be any old letter that I've ripped up."

Avery could see it in her friend's eyes. She was beginning to wonder if Avery had made the entire thing up. They'd had arguments like that before when they were kids, and Tiffany had that same look now.

"I'm sorry," Avery relented. "I didn't mean to snap at you like that. I'm just not sleeping well, and I'm really stressed about it all."

Tiffany took the dog's lead from Avery and helped to pry him away from the cellar door. Sprinkles put up a decent fight, too. He seemed adamant that he stay at the door and bark at whatever it was that held his attention.

"That's alright," she said softly. "I can see that all of this is really affecting you. I just wish I knew how to help."

"I honestly don't know what to do," Avery admitted.

The women wrestled Sprinkles back toward the home, closing him inside for the night. Tiffany lit a fire for Avery and chose a combination of movies for her to watch to keep her mind off of it all.

"You need to get some sleep Avery," Tiffany said with a kind smile. "You can't expect to survive any day, the good or the bad if you don't have proper rest."

"Yes, ma'am," Avery answered sarcastically.

Then, Tiffany left and Avery was once again alone in her own home. It was starting to feel like torture to her when she was there alone. Every sound made her jump, and farmhouses always had a lot of sounds once the sun had set.

Every time she had to open the door for Sprinkles to take a bathroom break, she braced herself, wondering if she'd be faced with the person who had written her that threatening letter. Her nerve endings were feeling completely frayed, and she wished she could run away.

But she had nowhere else to go. She couldn't face the city again, and her husband's funeral arrangements had nearly cleared out all her savings. She couldn't run away.

So, she made herself comfortable on the couch, with every table lamp turned on, and picked out a romantic comedy from the list of movies that Tiffany had selected.

As she watched the movie and sipped her wine, she contemplated how simple things seemed to the characters on the screen. It made her remember when she'd met her husband. Every bride she'd ever known had been so convinced that it would be forever, and she had been no different on her wedding day.

Yet, at forty-five years old, she sat alone and without her husband. They had planned their entire lives together, and she had never thought about what she would do if he was no longer around.

They were supposed to grow old together like her parents and grandparents had. The most she had ever expected her or James to have to live without each other was only a year or two, at the age of ninety-nine.

She had always seen herself as a strong and independent woman. But that was not how she felt as she sat on the couch, crying at the cuteness of how the movie had ended. She was far from strong. She was terrified and had no idea what to do about it.

Avery was once again drifting into a dream world. She knew she had to be dreaming because when she looked down at her hands they were not hers. They were her mother's hands. It was a nightmare.

And she was mad about it. She had made nearly five cups of coffee in an attempt to stay awake. Right before she'd drifted off, she'd decided that she'd rather sleep in the day when the farm was busy. It was a foolish decision to go to sleep, and she knew better. But she did it anyway.

As she walked across the lawn, her feet kicked up clouds of fog. The fog was so thick that she couldn't see her feet at all. She could hear Sprinkles barking at the cellar door, and she had his lead in her hands.

She wasn't sure how she got to be halfway across the lawn, but she knew she was on her way to fetch Sprinkles. The morning sun was rising, and soon the fog would clear, and she'd need to get to work on the farm. She looked around to judge what the weather would bring.

But she was met with an awful sight. The vines were dead and decaying. Sticking out from the frost were gray, gnarled branches, but they had grown higher than her head. It was clear they hadn't had fruit for years. The dead vineyard seemed to stretch out for miles and miles.

"Unbelievable," she whispered.

Avery detoured, stepping closer to the dead vineyard to understand what the cause of death might have been. She'd read every book on vineyard diseases and disasters, and nothing had ever looked like that.

When she reached out and touched the vine, it crumbled beneath her fingers into nothing but ash that floated away on the soft breeze.

"That's not possible," she whispered.

The sound of Sprinkles barking drew her attention away again. Without taking another step, she found herself in front of the cellar door, the soft fur of her puppy brushing up against her leg.

"What has gotten into you?" she asked. "Let's get you inside."

Before Avery could bend down to attach his lead, a single knock came from inside the cellars. Her heart was pounding as she stared at the door, listening for any sign of life on the other side. Sprinkles had also fallen completely silent, and she could no longer feel his fur against her leg.

"H-hello?" she called softly.

Another loud bang from inside the cellar sent her stumbling backward with fright. Avery fell over Sprinkles, who had been hiding behind her, and fell onto the soft, damp grass. She looked up just as the door to the cellar swung open.

She knew who it was even before he spoke. She recognized

him from the dream she'd had before. This time, she felt prepared.

"I'm not going in there," she said sternly. "So don't waste your time asking."

But instead of the angry cursing she'd received before, she heard a soft whimper from the man.

"Please," he cried softly. "You have to help me."

It was even more unsettling than when he was angry. His tall body was bent over as he buried his face in his hands, and he stumbled slightly over his own footing as he walked. But for every step he took forward, Avery scrambled backward away from him.

"I cannot rest," he cried. "You need to get them to listen. You need to do something."

"I-I don't know what you want me to do," Avery answered, sliding further and further away from him.

The form of Mr. Grier lifted his head from his hands and looked at her. His face was thin, pale, and covered in red streaks from the crying.

"Trust your gut," he said. "Please, trust your gut and help me."

At that point, Avery stopped crawling away and stared up at him in disbelief. He had stopped walking, too. Instead, he looked out over the dead vineyard.

"This is all I am now," he said, gesturing to his surroundings.

Before Avery could say another word, Mr. Grier collapsed. When his body hit the ground, it turned into a cloud of ash. The dead vines around Avery also collapsed, and soon, the gray, dead ash of her family's vineyard consumed her.

～

When Avery startled awake, it was because Sprinkles was yet again barking at the cellar door. She had been so confused by the dream and was so stiff from sleeping on the couch again that she was hardly paying any attention to anything else.

"How did you get out?" she asked nobody in particular as she searched desperately for the keys to the door.

Avery pulled the door open and ran outside to get the dog. She couldn't stand his barking anymore. She wanted nothing more to do with the cellar.

But she hadn't noticed that it was already light outside. The sun had already evaporated the morning dew on the lawn when Avery rushed out, wearing nothing but her underwear and t-shirt.

Chapter Ten

"Oof!"

That was the sound that Charles made when Avery came crashing into him, only half-dressed. A loud thud followed as the two of them tumbled onto the lawn. It all completely discombobulated Avery. Charles rolled over, making sure to keep his eyes off her as she tried desperately to scramble to her feet.

It was likely too late, though, and she knew he had probably seen her. He had been facing the house when she had come running out. She had been in such a daze that she hadn't even realized it was morning yet.

"I'm so sorry!" she mumbled as she raced back towards the house.

"Don't worry about it," he groaned.

She'd hit him hard and was certain that the force of her body had knocked the wind out of him completely.

She hadn't even given him a moment to get a word in. As soon as she had crossed the boundary into her home, she slammed the door behind her and let out a loud sigh.

Without a mirror, she knew that her cheeks were bright pink from embarrassment.

It was dark inside, with all the curtains still closed, but she couldn't get herself to open them. That would risk making eye contact with Charles, who she could hear was busy getting Sprinkles away from the cellar door.

She had heard him laugh a little, and she had no idea if he was laughing at the situation or at the sight of her. She was certain her hair was a mess, and she was wearing the oldest shirt she had in her closet.

It was one of James' shirts, and it already had a few holes in it when she had inherited it. It was the only one comfortable enough to sleep in.

Avery washed the embarrassment off as she showered, got dressed, and helped herself to a hot cup of coffee. She'd planned to meet the women of the Stammtisch that day. Initially, she had thought about canceling, but after her run-in with Charles, she figured it was a good excuse to get away from any further potential embarrassment.

Fully dressed and with her largest pair of sunglasses on, Avery made her way to the car. She had hoped to avoid everyone on the way there, but she wasn't quite so lucky.

"Avery!" Charles called before she could open the car door. "Wait a second!"

She sighed and forced a smile before turning to meet him.

"Hi, Charles," she greeted. "Sorry about this morning."

Charles let out an awkward chuckle. "No worries," he said. "I was headed that way to give you something. This arrived for you late yesterday."

He handed her an envelope, and immediately her heart sank. It looked just like the one from the previous letter, and the handwriting on the front of the envelope was the same.

She didn't want to take it. She wished she could run away from him again.

"I think it's the same as last time," Charles said. "Looks like the same writing, doesn't it?"

Avery fiddled nervously with the envelope for a moment before losing patience and tearing it open. Her hands shook as she folded the letter open to read it.

I warned you once. Stop talking. Don't go to the police. Or you'll pay the price.

This is your final warning.

She felt like she might be sick as she read it a few more times. Whoever was sending the letters knew she had been to the police. Charles grabbed the letter from her and read it through, stretching his eyes wide as he read.

"Please tell me you've had some luck with the guest book?" Avery asked.

Charles shook his head. "Hardly anybody is willing to leave a comment," he said, sounding completely defeated. "What are you going to do?"

Avery shrugged. "I think I'm just going to forget about it and pretend like none of it ever happened," she answered. "I'm already in over my head."

Charles didn't look impressed with that answer, but she didn't care. She had no energy left for any of it. Besides, whatever had happened or was going on at that point, it really was none of her business.

"I've gotta go," she said before Charles could change her mind.

~

Avery stared at the small tastings of wine in front of her. She hadn't taken a single sip yet. She wasn't sure she could stomach it. Avery had lost track of the conversation entirely. On her drive over to Eleanor's house, she had decided not to talk about it. She was fully prepared to leave the entire case behind her.

It left her with an unexpected feeling of longing. She hadn't realized that while investigating the case, she'd had a familiar feeling. It was as if she had been working on one of her husband's crime novels again. It had always been one of her favorite things to do, and this case had made her feel like that again. But it wasn't one of his books. It was real life, and she was potentially in some real trouble, and he wasn't there.

The mix of emotions was making it nearly impossible for her to keep track of the conversation. She laughed when the others laughed, and that was about it.

"What's going on, Avery?" Deb asked.

They were all looking at her. Avery felt small and defeated, and she had no idea how to explain it all to them in a way that made sense. But they were waiting for an answer. She had to think fast.

"I'm just very tired, that's all," she lied. "I didn't sleep well last night."

"No," Deb said with a suspicious look on her face. "You've been tired since we met you. This seems like something else."

"Yeah, you've hardly said a word since you arrived," Camille added. "You haven't even had a single sip of wine!"

Avery's mind raced as she tried her best to come up with a believable lie. But she couldn't. She could think of nothing other than the letter she'd received earlier that day. With trembling fingers, she reached into her bag and revealed the note.

The women gasped. Eleanor reached out and snatched it

from Avery's hand, and the others jumped to join her as they read it in unison.

"You have to go to the police," Camille insisted. "This note is still intact!"

"She can't do that!" Eleanor argued. "Didn't you read the letter? It says not to!"

"Well, then, what are you going to do?" Camille asked, looking up at Avery. "You can't do nothing."

Avery shook her head. She explained about both of the terrible dreams she'd had about Mr. Grier. She told them that Charles hadn't had any luck trying to match the handwriting. She told them about the dog barking at the cellar door.

The more she spoke, the more absurd it all seemed. The town was so small that surely there couldn't be such heavy secrets.

"Should I move?" Avery eventually asked, exasperated.

Eleanor leaned back in her chair and thought for a moment. Then she snapped her fingers and leaned forward.

"I bet this is a prank," she said. "Just like we said before."

"Do you really think so?" Avery responded.

"Yeah!" Eleanor said cheerfully. "I mean, think about it. If someone really wanted to threaten you, they wouldn't do it this way and certainly not twice...I don't think."

The women thought about it for a moment before they agreed. It didn't make Avery feel any better, though. Whether it was a prank or not, it was unpleasant receiving threats like that, and she hated the thought that perhaps her entire life was being disrupted by the handy work of a bored teenager.

"Look, you're far too stressed out," Camille added. "Why don't we help you clean out the rest of the cellar? Then you can put your mind at ease."

"That's a great idea!" Deb chimed in. "We can have music and snacks and make a whole day of it!"

"I'm in!" Eleanor added with a smile.

Avery had never expected the women to care that much about her well-being. Could it be possible that she was making real friends for the first time in her adult life?

"This sounds like fun!" Deb sang as she poured herself another glass of wine.

Her new friends had somehow taken a situation that was entirely too stressful for Avery to handle and turned it into something fun and exciting.

"Thank you," Avery smiled.

With that, the women agreed they would meet early the next day to clean out the remainder of the cellar.

That night, with the knowledge that help was on its way in the morning, Avery slept deeply and easily through the night.

Chapter Eleven

Avery sat at home and thought about the upcoming cleaning party. The women of the Stammtisch had decided that they would turn it into something positive and fun. One of them had even curated a playlist, and Avery had divided the tasks up between the four of them. It should only take a few hours for them to clear the cellar completely.

Knowing that she had the support of her new friends behind her, she felt a new confidence swell inside her. She refused to be taken down by a bored teenager. With a new spring in her step, she loaded all her evidence into her car and headed to the police station.

"You're back," one of the officers said with a bored look on his face. "And you've brought the suitcase with you again."

Avery slammed the suitcase on the counter, along with the original note she'd found in the cellar.

"Look, lady, I thought I told you. We can't accept this," the officer complained.

Avery smiled. "I've got more."

She handed the police officer the document that proved

the blood match to Mr. Grier. He looked through the document with a puzzled look on his face.

"It says a blood match," he mumbled. "But I'm not exactly sure which blood you've matched the man to."

Avery sighed and pushed the suitcase closer to him. "See these drops on the case? That was our sample."

The officer looked at the droplets on the case and back to the blood analysis report.

"How exactly did you get this?" he asked, waving the page around.

"That's not important," Avery said. "It's from a reputable source, and it's further evidence."

The policeman sighed loudly and rolled his eyes.

"Look, lady," he said, leaning forward on the counter. "As I've said before you've got no proof of where you found this. That blood could come from everywhere. You have nothing that suggests the suitcase and the note are connected. This means nothing."

Avery smiled. "If it means nothing, then why am I receiving threats?" she asked, sliding the most recent letter across the counter.

He lifted the letter and read through it a few times.

"Let me guess," he sighed. "This arrived in the dead of night, and nobody was there to see it arrive, and I'm just supposed to believe you."

"Actually, that arrived in the mail, delivered in broad daylight by the postman. So there are a few witnesses to that," she answered. "Besides, why would I make this entire thing up?"

The officer shrugged. "I dunno. It's a small town. People get bored."

"I've got better things to do than that," she scoffed. "Anyway, I'm not leaving here until you take this in as evidence. I can't live with it in my home anymore. I'm perfectly willing to give a written statement."

"Have you considered that this letter is just a prank?" the officer asked condescendingly.

"Yes," Avery chirped. "But until we have proof that it is a prank, all it possibly could be is a threat. I intend to treat it as such, and so should you. That's your job, I believe?"

With that remark, another nearby officer who'd been listening in snorted a little as he tried to conceal a chuckle. The other officer got up and walked up to the counter.

"I've got this one," he said, taking the items from Avery. "Hello, ma'am. My name is Officer Matthews."

Officer Matthews was an older gentleman. Avery guessed that he probably should have retired years ago already.

Avery let out a sigh of relief. Finally, someone was willing to help her. Officer Matthews took great care listing all the items out on a form and writing detailed descriptions of it all. Then, he handed her a pen and paper and allowed her to write out a lengthy description of everything that had happened over the last few weeks. And she spared no detail either.

When she was done, she handed it all back to him and thanked him profusely for his help.

"You know, I always thought it odd when your parents got the farm instead of the Cutters. It was a big deal around here," he said as he logged her report.

"What do you mean?" she asked, pausing at the door.

Officer Matthews shrugged. "Well, when Mr. Grier disappeared, the Cutters had put down a large sum of money to buy his property. Your parents came out of nowhere, with much less money, and bought the property out from under them."

Avery had never heard that version of events before.

Then again, it never would have been something that would have come up in conversation. She had moved to the farm while she was still quite young.

"I remember it being quite the talk of the town at the time," he added.

Avery thanked the officer and headed home. Already she felt quite a bit lighter knowing that someone had accepted the items into evidence. She couldn't stand having them around her home anymore. The only thing she hadn't given them was the first letter she'd received. It had been torn into too many parts. She realized it was unlikely they would accept it.

Still, the information about the Cutters bothered her. The farm was great, but only because her parents had put in the work. It certainly wasn't anything worth fighting for when they moved there. Why would the Cutters be so interested in the property?

As soon as she got home, she went straight to her parent's cottage at the end of the property.

"What brings you here?" her mother asked as she poured a cup of tea.

"I was chatting to Officer Matthews earlier, and he told me that the Cutters had originally put an offer on this property," Avery explained.

"Officer Matthews?" her father asked. "What were you down at the police station for?"

Avery didn't have the energy to explain everything that had happened to them. She had chosen to keep them somewhat in the dark about it all. They were too concerned about her, and she knew they would just try to get too involved.

"I had some admin stuff to wrap up," she said, telling a partial truth. "He mentioned it was quite a scandal when you bought the farm."

Her parents laughed together.

"I can't believe they're still talking about it," her mother chuckled. "It really wasn't that big of a deal."

"Not to us!" her father joked. "We got the farm!"

"Yeah," Avery said. "But I believe their offer was much larger than yours. So how did you manage to purchase the farm in the end?"

Avery's mother sat down at the table and joined her for tea. She sipped her tea slowly and smiled at Avery. Her mother had always had a way of making her wait for the answer to a question. It had always driven Avery nuts.

"Mr. Grier was the cousin of your grandmother," she explained. "So, we didn't originally know this, but Mr. Grier had some or other clause in his will that should something happen to him, the family had the first choice over the property."

"Yeah," her father chimed in. "It didn't really matter how much money the Cutters had ready to pay as long as we covered the debt owed, the property was ours for the taking."

"Nobody else in the family wanted it," her mother shrugged.

"Why didn't anybody else want it?" Avery asked. "I mean, surely somebody else was also interested? If even for sentimental value?"

"Mr. Grier wasn't exactly the most pleasant person," her father said. "I remember my mother telling me about how all the children found him frightening. He hardly ever smiled."

"Yeah," her mother agreed. "Nobody really knew him very well at all. And the farm wasn't in the greatest condition. I suppose you could say we were the only ones in the family brave enough."

"There's just something that bothers me," Avery added.

"If the property was in such bad condition, why would the Cutters offer so much money to buy it?"

Her father shrugged. "At the time, the Cutters were buying almost every farm that became available," he explained. "They had some dream to start this wine empire of theirs here, and I guess they wanted to scare anybody else off from putting down an offer."

"I didn't know Mr. Grier was technically family of ours," Avery said.

"Well, he was a loner," her mother explained. "Nobody really knew him. He bought the farm when he was young and had lived here ever since. Even his parents never heard from him. They received the occasional Christmas card. That's why it took so long for anyone to even notice that he was missing."

"When the news finally did reach us, we jumped at the opportunity to buy the property," her father continued. "It was the perfect place for us to start our business and raise our beautiful child."

Chapter Twelve

The new information about the property seemed to make sense to Avery. There was only one thing that she did not quite understand.

"Mr. Grier was never pronounced dead," she said as she placed her teacup back on the saucer. "So how could his will be in effect?"

"That's where it got a little tricky," her father laughed. "Since he wasn't dead, we had to sign a clause that if he ever returned, we would hand the property back to him. It would be back in his name, and we'd have to sort it out with him. We simply have responsibility for the property in the meantime."

Avery nearly choked on her tea. It seemed absurd. It was an insane risk for parents to take. She remembered how they had packed up and left everything behind to live on the farm.

"How did you know he wouldn't come back?" she asked. "We would have lost everything!"

Her mother raised her eyebrows and sighed. "We were just certain he wouldn't."

That was it. That was her entire explanation for how they were able to take such a large risk. She imagined what might have happened if he had come back. They would have been left entirely without a home to live in. In a flash, she wondered what they might have done if that had happened and how different her life might have been if they'd been forced to leave the farm.

"How could you be so certain, though?" she asked.

Her father laughed. "He really wasn't well-liked. The community had made it clear to him that it wasn't fond of him...why would he come back?"

"And you guys are certain he's still alive?"

It seemed like a stupid question, but they seemed so certain that he wouldn't be back that she just had to ask it, even if it was only to put her mind at ease.

"We're pretty certain," her father answered.

But she wasn't quite convinced enough yet.

"What's with all the questions?" he asked. "You've never shown an interest in any of this before."

Avery never got the chance to answer. The way her parents filled every available pause with speaking made her realize that she should probably visit them more often.

"Look," her father said, "there was never any evidence that he'd died. Besides, when we'd moved in I found a safe in the back of the spare room cupboard. It was open, and it was clear a large sum of money had been taken from it."

"How do you know?" she pressed.

Avery could see that her father was getting frustrated with her, but it was the most information she'd been able to get on Mr. Grier since they'd moved to the farm. At that point, she felt she deserved to know more about him.

"There was a ledger in there where he'd kept a record of how much money went in and out of the safe at any given time," he said. "So I could see how much was supposed to be in there. And it wasn't there. It was definitely opened with the key too."

"Happy?" her mother asked.

"No," Avery mumbled. "If he was such a loner, why would he keep a ledger of how much money was in the safe? If he was the only one living here, then he'd know how much was there because he was the only one taking from it."

Her father thought it over for a moment and sighed. "As I said, he was a strange man."

"That he was," her mother added. "He left almost everything behind. It took us weeks to sort through all of his personal belongings. Still to this day, I find boxes of his stuff everywhere."

"So, if he isn't dead. Then where do you think he went?" Avery asked.

"This is the most conversation we've had in weeks," her mother complained. "Why are you so interested in all of this, anyway?"

"I don't know," Avery said, pouring herself another cup of tea. "I guess up until now, he's just been a name that I knew of. Now he seems to be a real person, and it's interesting to me."

"Well, I think he just found somewhere better to be," her father chimed in. "Let's be honest. He was no good at owning a vineyard. The place needed some more care."

"That's right!" her mother laughed. "I think he found a small home somewhere nice and quiet and went on and became happy with his life."

"Well, why not just sell the farm then?" Avery asked. "He could have used the money."

"That takes time," her father explained. "Besides, you're thinking way too logically about someone who was never a very logical man."

"Ain't that the truth," her mother agreed. "I remember

your grandmother telling me how he used to try to parachute off the roof with little plastic baggies. He was a strange kid and an even stranger adult."

Avery thought it over for a moment. It seemed like a harsh judgment. She could remember many times when she had considered the plastic-bag-parachute experiment as a kid. The only reason she never really followed through with it was that her parents would have grounded her.

They had really painted the picture that he was a particularly unwelcome man but without giving any real reason why. She wondered what she might have done in his situation. If the entire town had decided that they no longer liked her, would she have stayed? Or would she have left too?

"Why exactly didn't the town like him?" she asked, desperate to ease her curiosity about it all.

"They thought he was a strange man," her mother replied.

"Oh, come on, Mom," she argued. "It can't be that simple. You don't get shunned by an entire town for being a little odd."

"He was an imbecile!" her father commented from the sidelines. "He ran this place into the ground."

Her mother shot him a glare that quickly made him keep quiet. Her father had a habit of commenting from the sidelines, which drove her mother mad. All their marriage, they had butted heads over it. And yet, there was never a compromise. It had taught Avery early on that people are who they are and that change is a choice.

"That's beside the point," she said slowly. "They didn't shun him because of what he did to the vineyard. They felt he was unfriendly. He would go wine tasting at the other farms and scare away the customers with his anti-social behavior!"

"He never had any friends either," her father added. "He never showed interest in socializing with anyone either."

"Yeah, so nobody trusted him," her mother said. "In a town like this, you have to make friends. People want to know who you are and what you're about. Then they trust you!"

"They blamed him for the drop in tourism, too," her father continued. "His farm was getting terrible reviews, so people stopped visiting here and went to the other towns."

"Alright, I get it," Avery laughed. "He sounds like a really difficult person to deal with."

"People had made offers to buy the farm. He'd refused every single one of them. Quite rudely, I might add," her mother said.

"That's odd," Avery whispered. "If he was unwilling to sell the farm, then why'd he just leave it behind? It doesn't make any sense."

"That's because you're trying to make sense of something completely nonsensical," her father chirped. "Like trying to catch smoke with a net."

"The Cutters had hated him the most of all," her mother continued. "That's after he apparently accidentally set fire to one of their plants. He was sneaking a cigarette where he shouldn't have been. Granted, the fire wasn't very big. Tiny even, but they hated him for it nonetheless. They had it in their heads that he had done it on purpose. It was preposterous."

"I'll never understand why they were so eager to buy this farm," her father said, deep in thought. "You'd think they'd want nothing to do with it judging by the way they talk about him."

"So why do you think he left?" Avery asked, her face scrunched up into a tight frown.

"Perhaps he just grew tired of all the politics," her father answered. "What do they call it? A nervous breakdown or something."

"I think he met someone and ran off with them to be somewhere happier," her mother said with a smile. "Although I don't know who on Earth could possibly have the patience for someone like that."

"One thing is for sure," her mother continued. "He's had plenty of time to come back, and nobody's ever heard so much as a peep from him. I don't know where he is or why he left, but I am pretty certain he's never coming back."

"He might have died by now for all we know," her father added. "He would be quite the elderly gentleman by now too."

Avery thanked her parents for the tea and made her way back home. She needed to rest in preparation for the cleaning party the next day. With more information about Mr. Grier, she couldn't get him out of her mind. The more she thought about it, the more questions she had. None of it made sense, and none of her parents' answers made much sense either. They simply weren't good enough for her.

She looked at him as if he was a character in one of James' books. Why would he have left? Where would he have gone? Why didn't he come back?

Chapter Thirteen

Music played loudly throughout the cellar as the team, including Dr. Moses, got to work cleaning out the rest of the cellar. Avery was grateful for the help. Everybody seemed excited about the task at hand. It seemed lighter in the cellar than it ever had before when Avery was cleaning alone.

It was as if every bad feeling she'd had about the space had disappeared completely.

From the back of the cellar, Avery heard a yelp coming from Deb. The group stopped to see what the problem was as a pale-faced Deb came trotting out from one of the side rooms.

"Dr. Moses," she said, out of breath. "There's a creature of some kind back there. Do you think you could get it?"

"A creature?" he asked with suspicion. "Does it have fur?"

Deb nodded. "And big floppy bunny ears."

"So, it's a bunny?" Dr. Moses asked, leaning against the broom.

"It certainly looks like one," Deb answered. "I'm really

not good with animals. I have no pets at home. Could you please come and get it out?"

"I can't!" Dr. Moses answered, much to everybody's shock. "I'm allergic to furry animals, and I haven't taken my antihistamine today."

There was a stunned silence for a moment as everyone waited for him to start laughing. But the longer they waited, the more they realized he wasn't joking.

"But you're a vet!" Camille cried as she bubbled with laughter.

"That I am!" Dr. Moses agreed. "Most days, I take an antihistamine. This morning, however, I forgot. And I'm already taking a big enough risk being in the room with Sprinkles. I'm sorry, guys, I can't touch the rabbit. Not unless any of you have an antihistamine with you."

Avery could hear them tease him relentlessly about it as she left to rummage through her first aid kit for an antihistamine. But by the time she'd returned empty-handed, Eleanor already had the bunny by its front paws and was carrying it out towards the bushes for release.

She waited for Eleanor to return before walking with her to join the others.

"It really is a beautiful vineyard," Eleanor said as they entered the cellars. "You must be quite proud."

"Apparently, it didn't always look like this," Avery responded. "My parents were telling me about it yesterday. It was in terrible shape when they bought it, but it seemed to be pretty sought after, so I suppose it always had potential."

"What do you mean it was sought after?" Eleanor asked.

"I learned yesterday that the Cutters had put down a relatively large offer on the property, but since my family was related to Mr. Grier and due to some obscure clause, they were able to buy it for less."

"The Cutters wanted to buy the place?" Dr. Moses asked.

Avery nodded. "Apparently, they were trying to start some kind of wine empire out here."

"They do own most of the vineyards around here," Camille added. "They must have been pretty mad when your parents got the place. The Cutters always get what they want. They're a particularly tenacious family."

"How badly do you think they wanted the farm?" Deb asked with a sinister smile. "Badly enough to...murder for it?"

She was teasing, of course, but it set off a conspiracy amongst the group as they cleaned. They imagined all the ways the Cutters could have arranged for Mr. Grier's demise so that they could buy his property.

"Imagine how frustrated you must be if you arrange for someone's murder, with the idea of taking their land...and then somebody else still buys it because of some strange legal loophole," Eleanor laughed.

"Has anyone seen the Cutter's handwriting lately?" Camille teased. "Perhaps it's a match!"

"Good heavens, no," Dr. Moses added. "The Cutters are so old now, they can't see well enough to write any note by hand. The last time they brought their pet in for a consultation with me, they brought me the wrong dog!"

"What do you think happened to old Mr. Grier?" Deb finally asked, looking a little more serious.

Avery shrugged. "I don't know. Maybe my parents were right. Maybe he was just a strange man and grew tired of the hatred he was receiving from the town and simply left to seek life elsewhere. According to my father, he took a great deal of money with him too."

"What about the suitcase and the note?" Dr. Moses

asked, looking almost disappointed that the case had come to an end.

"Perhaps it's just an odd coincidence," Avery answered. "The note could be about anything, and from what I understand, Mr. Grier really was an odd man. Odd enough to stash his favorite clothes somewhere underneath the floorboards and cut his finger while boarding it back up."

"I suppose that does make some kind of sense," Eleanor agreed. "Besides, there's never been a murder in this town ever. It's just simply not a very violent place."

"Perhaps the note was merely someone confirming that he'd finally left the town," Dr. Moses chirped.

"But what about the threats you've been receiving?" Camille asked, concerned.

"Deb was obviously blabbing all over town!" Eleanor teased. "The kids here get bored. It's exactly the kind of prank I would have pulled when I was younger."

There was a collaborative nod as the group debunked all the things that had created so much stress before. As they cleaned away the dust in the cellar, Avery emptied her mind of paranoia. With the help of her new friends, she was able to let go of her concerns.

With progress being made in the cellar, she finally felt like things were coming into place for her again, and it was only giving her the itch to keep going. She considered for a moment that perhaps her new friends would help her clean out her home too.

She didn't like the idea that there might still be some of Mr. Grier's items lurking around in her cupboards. It might not have bothered her parents, but she was determined to make the space her own. She was about to ask them for help when she was interrupted.

"Hey guys, come check this out," Dr. Moses called.

He was in the furthest room of the cellars. It was the

room the Sprinkles had usually been so concerned with. But Sprinkles was being kept away on account of Dr. Moses' allergies.

The group walked curiously closer to the room and peeked inside. It was a small room, and most of the rooms had been empty, apart from an old empty barrel here and there.

Initially, the back room looked no different. It was empty except for a barrel standing in the far corner. The barrel had a label on it.

"I tried to move it," Dr. Moses said. "It's full. It won't budge."

"You mean there's wine in there?" Avery asked in excitement.

Dr. Moses shrugged. "I guess."

The barrel was old, and the label was too faded to read. All she could make out was the name of the vineyard as it had been before her parents had bought it: *Vin de Maison.*

"That wine must be so old," Avery said under her breath. "It certainly won't be drinkable, but I'm curious to know about it."

"I wonder why this barrel was left behind," Deb said.

"Like I said, the farm was in bad condition," Avery responded. "If what I've been told is to be believed, then Mr. Grier really knew very little about vineyards, and this is exactly the kind of thing he would forget about."

"Should we move it?" Eleanor asked. "I'm sure if we all put our strength in, we could get it out of here."

"No," Avery answered. "I'm worried about the age of the barrel. It might break, and that would be one big, smelly mess. Let's clean around it; I'll figure out what to do about it later."

So, the crew continued on with their cleaning. The

music continued to filter through the room as they wiped away years and years' worth of dust and filth.

Avery had finally decided what she wanted to do with the rooms. She would turn them into bed and breakfast rooms. She would add life into the space that she once suspected had been the home of death. It felt so positive to her that she no longer felt any anxiety at all about the items that she had found. She was excited about the cellars that she had once been so fearful of. She'd had nightmares about the space, and now that it was cleaner and empty, she could decide a future for it. It was perfect.

The vineyard that had once been her escape from life was quickly becoming her purpose in life. Before, she'd never had a purpose without James. He had been her world and everything she'd always wanted. And she had once felt that her life meant nothing without him.

Not anymore.

Chapter Fourteen

It had only taken a few hours, but the cellars were finally clean and cleared of all junk, except for the one last barrel in the furthest room. The group had shared a bottle of wine to celebrate, and Avery had made sure to feed them all.

"You know, it's still early," Dr. Moses said, checking his watch. "I've cleared my entire day for this. Are you sure we can't help you remove that barrel from back there?"

Avery had actually given it some thought as they were finishing up the cleaning. And she was certain she had an idea that could work, but it seemed tedious.

"The best way to do it, without making too much mess, would be to tap the liquid out into buckets and get rid of it," she suggested. "Once the barrel is empty, I'll feel far more comfortable moving it out."

"How many buckets do you have?" Deb asked.

"Too many to count," Avery said with a sigh.

Deb thought about it for a moment. "I'll stay and help," she offered. "But then I want the bed and breakfast named after me."

With that, they decided they would tackle the last obstacle that stood in her way. They would empty the barrel and remove it from the space, leaving a blank canvas for Avery to play with. She'd never been more excited about work.

With their buckets ready, they headed into the back of the cellars and prepared themselves to tap the wine.

The tap on the barrel was older and was a bit stuck. But with some brute strength from Dr. Moses, they were able to get it open, and they waited eagerly for the liquid to come pouring out.

That's not what happened, though. Instead of old, gross, liquid wine, thick black sludge plopped out of the tap. A few sludgy bits fell into the first bucket, and then it stopped completely, and the tap was blocked.

The room filled with a found stench that had Camille dry-heaving into the neck of her sweater.

"What is that?" she cried. "That can't be wine!"

"No, I doubt it," Avery said, covering her nose with her hands.

"Where do you keep your tools?" Dr. Moses piped up. "I'll cut the top of the barrel off."

It took a while for Dr. Moses to get the task done. The smell was so rotten that he had to come out of the cellar regularly for fresh air. Avery had begged him not to continue she didn't want to be the reason he got ill. But he insisted he wanted the filthy barrel out of there.

Eleanor sighed. "Just let him do it."

When Dr. Moses appeared from the cellar with the top of the barrel in his hands, Avery covered her nose with a scarf and slowly entered back into the space with Dr. Moses following closely behind. Even with the scarves wrapped around her face, the smell was almost unbearable.

When she finally approached the barrel and peered

inside, it took her a moment to understand precisely what she was looking at. It was filled with dark, stinking sludge. Avery had never seen anything like it before.

On the surface were bits of material. The material was largely disintegrated into the sludge, but part of it seemed like a collar.

"What on Earth?" Avery asked as she leaned further over the barrel.

"Avery," Dr. Moses put his hand on her shoulder.

When Avery looked up at him and saw the look in his eyes, she immediately realized what she was looking at. When she looked down again, she spotted what looked like a piece of bone protruding out from the thick sludge.

Avery ran through the cellar toward the fresh air, her heart pounding rapidly in her chest. When she finally made it out, she fell to her knees and pulled the scarf from her face, worried that she'd be sick.

"What is it?" Eleanor asked as she rushed over to Avery.

But Avery couldn't answer. She was in shock and was certain that she would pass out at any moment.

"Talk to me, Avery," Eleanor demanded. "What's wrong?"

"There's a body in there," Dr. Moses said as he appeared from the cellars.

A wave of shock washed over the entire group as his words sunk in. Avery couldn't help but think of all the times James had written about moments just like that one. Only, it was so much worse than anything he'd ever written.

There were no cleverly chosen words and descriptions to ease her into it. There was only horror and stink and sludge. All her excitement came crashing down around her as she stared at the cellar door. The memory of her nightmares about Mr. Grier, the note, and the suitcase, came flooding back. She just sat and stared in disbelief.

Thankfully, she'd had friends with her.

~

The next few hours were a blur for Avery as she answered the same questions asked over and over again by varying police officers. People in suits, people with medical equipment, and people with cameras all flooded her vineyard. Soon, she wasn't allowed any access to the cellars at all.

"Do you believe me now?" she said to the police officer who'd rejected her attempts at handing in the evidence.

He had nothing to say to her. Instead, he just looked at her in disbelief, his mouth hanging open like a fish out of water. So, she turned her attention to Officer Matthews.

"Have you looked into the Cutters yet?" she asked. "They hated him. They wanted the farm for themselves."

"Avery," Officer Matthews said kindly. "I understand that this is stressful and you're afraid. But we're doing the best that we can."

"What about the threat I received?" she asked with tears in her eyes. "I might be in real danger. It might be my body in the barrel next."

He smiled. "We won't let that happen. I promise."

The sun was already setting by the time the police had wrapped up their questioning. Avery greeted her friends as they all went home to recover from the horrific experience. It was only her and a few police officers left.

"You need to get some rest," Officer Matthews said, placing a friendly hand on her shoulder.

"How can you expect me to sleep?" she asked. "There's a murderer out there who knows I've exposed them. I can't sleep!"

Officer Matthews sighed. "Let me make some phone calls,"

he said kindly. "Tell you what. I'll stay posted outside your house tonight. And we'll make sure there's an officer here all the time until we're certain that there's no threat. Is that alright?"

Avery gave him a short nod as she wiped away tears. It wasn't the ideal situation, but it's what she had. And she had nowhere else to go. It didn't matter how many officers kept watch outside her home that night. She knew she wouldn't be getting any sleep.

A few days had passed when Avery got the first bits of information from the police investigation. She had dark rings under her eyes as she squinted at her computer screen to read the email that had come through.

Avery,

I want to keep you updated on the current investigation regarding the dead body found on your property. We wish that we could tell you more, but most of our leads have walked us directly to a dead-end.

Two things are clear in this investigation:

1. The Cutters were abroad at the time of the murder and at the time of Mr. Grier's disappearance. This clears them of all suspicion.

2. The body that was in the barrel is not a match for Mr. Grier. The body found in the barrel belonged to a woman.

We hope you are keeping well and safe. We hope to have more news for you soon.

Kindest regards,
Officer Matthews

Avery slumped back in her chair. It wasn't very good news at all. They were nowhere near solving the case, and that meant that her life was still at risk. She'd been sleeping mostly in one-hour batches throughout the day. It was enough sleep to keep her alive but not enough to feel fully rested.

Thankfully, they had kept to their promise and had made sure that an officer was stationed outside her house at all times. Soon, she would know them all by name and know everything about their families.

She'd been too fearful to go into town, so she'd been spending most of her time bothering the officers with pointless conversations in an attempt to keep herself distracted.

Avery wished that she could run away, just like Mr. Grier had. Disappearing, never to be seen again, was starting to sound more and more enticing to her. But she had nowhere else to go. And she couldn't do anything about any of it.

Chapter Fifteen

There were scuff marks forming on the floor where Avery had spent days pacing up and down. She could hardly sleep anymore. Every time she closed her eyes, she saw the image of that thick black sludge as it plopped out of the barrel's tap.

She barely spoke to anyone anymore. All they wanted to talk about was the event and how she was doing. It was becoming a boring conversation to her. She couldn't read a book because then she ran the risk of falling asleep and having another nightmare. It was the same risk with the television.

Avery slowed her pacing, straightening the artwork on the wall as she walked. There was some sun coming in through a crack in the curtains, but she kept them closed. She wasn't entirely comfortable with the officers being able to peer into her house at any moment. She preferred her privacy.

She was expecting her father to arrive any minute. It was his turn to drop off the groceries and check in on Avery.

And like clockwork, there was a knock at the door. It made Avery jump as it pulled her from her thoughts.

"Hi, Dad," she greeted as she opened the door.

He raised his bushy eyebrows and looked her up and down.

"You don't look so good," he said. "Did you get any sleep last night?"

Avery shook her head. "Don't tell Mom. As far as she's concerned, I'm in great condition."

Her father chuckled. "You got it."

He stepped into the house and marched towards the kitchen to put the groceries down. He paused for a moment and looked around.

"This place is spotless," he commented, running his fingers over the top of one of the shelves.

"Well, I haven't had much else to do," Avery said quietly as she started putting the groceries away.

Avery brewed a fresh pot of coffee for the two of them, and they sat at the kitchen table just as they used to when she was younger. They had always woken up much before her mother and had often sat in exactly the same spots and had meaningful conversations.

"How are you doing, Avery?" he asked. "Really, really."

Avery sighed. "I'm not sleeping very well," she said, rubbing her eyes. "And I've had a headache all morning. But I suppose I'm as alright as I can be."

Her father's shoulders slumped. "I wish there was something I could do."

Avery was about to answer when they were interrupted.

"Is there another one of those cups of coffee available?" Charles asked.

Avery nodded and poured him a cup, and he joined them at the table. The three sat in silence for a few minutes as they enjoyed their coffee until Avery recognized the unmistakable sound of her father's last slurp.

"Well," he said, smacking his lips. "I better go."

He greeted them both and left the house, leaving Avery and Charles alone at the table. It was a long silence before Charles finally spoke.

"I've been worried about you," he said, taking Avery by surprise.

"Really?" she asked with a chuckle. "I'm alright. But I understand now why you retired from your job. I don't ever want to see something like that ever again."

Charles snorted a little. "Trust me," he said. "In all my years of service, I'd never seen anything quite that gruesome."

Charles had gone pale in the face just from the thought of it, and the sight of him had made Avery laugh. It was the first time she'd really laughed in days, and it made her feel a little better.

"Is there anything I can do for you?" he asked. "Have you heard from the police?"

"Yeah," Avery sighed. "They don't have any answers. Only that the body in the barrel isn't Mr. Grier."

Charles leaned forward and stretched his eyes open wide. She could see the gears turning in his head as he processed the new information. She knew how he felt. She'd been just as convinced that Mr. Grier was the body in the barrel. It had been the only thing that she'd been fairly certain about.

"And the letters?" he continued. "Do they know who's been threatening you?"

She shook her head. "Nothing yet on that. So, I remain at home with armed guards posted outside."

Charles shook his head. "I'd be happy to keep an eye as well," he said with a smile.

"I couldn't ask that of you," she answered. "It's too much. Why would you offer something like that?"

Charles shrugged. "I care about you," he said. "You've always taken good care of me. You're an excellent boss. I owe your family and this farm so much. I'd be happy to do it."

Avery thought it over. He had been a cop before, and she certainly trusted Charles more than most.

"That would be great," she said with a smile. "It might be nice to have someone familiar around for a while."

"Then it will be arranged," he said, lifting himself from his chair. "Oh, and please open up some curtains?"

Charles smiled at her and left to make a phone call, and a few minutes later, the policeman left, and Charles took his place. Immediately Avery felt more at ease. There was something about Charles that was calming to her. He had a relaxed energy about him, which was just what she needed.

Plus, without the uniform, she could pretend he was just a friend hanging out on the patio. It helped her forget just a little bit that her life was actually in danger. With the person standing guard outside her house no longer a police-man, she opened some of the curtains and let the light in. And for the first time in a while, she was able to sleep for a few hours.

Avery woke up confused. It was the most sleep she'd had in days, and for a moment, she had no idea where she was. Eventually, she recognized the old green clock on the wall and knew that she was in her old childhood bedroom. When she saw the time, she couldn't believe how long she'd been asleep, and she woke up with new energy. The only problem with that was that she would likely not sleep at all that night. And she had no idea how to use all the energy she'd regenerated.

When her stomach growled, Avery was reminded that it'd been a while since her last meal. She was hungry but didn't have much of an appetite with all that had been on her mind lately. With newfound energy to burn, she decided to start preparing her mom's old beef stew recipe that she could eat later for dinner. Avery knew that smelling the stew cooking for hours would convince her to eat despite her lack of appetite.

While the stew cooked, Avery walked aimlessly through the house until she stopped in front of a long line of cupboards in the spare room. She hadn't paid them any attention since she'd moved in, but she knew that they needed attention.

When she'd moved in, her parents had made a point of telling her that they'd never gotten around to sorting out the spare room cupboards. It was hard to believe. It seemed almost impossible, in fact. But she remembered how they'd always spoken about it but never done it.

As a kid, she'd always been curious to know what was inside the cupboards, but her parents never let her look. The cupboards stretched all the way from one wall to the other and from the ceiling to the floor. Young Avery had always thought that there would be treasures hidden inside.

"If you open it, we'll have to sort it!" they used to joke.

As an adult, the cupboards just made her feel like there was a heavy weight on her shoulders. She didn't want to live with whatever was inside there anymore. She wanted to start new, and that meant getting rid of anything old.

"Time to sort you out," she whispered.

With some large boxes and trash bags at her disposal, she pulled open the doors and assessed the situation. The cupboards were full of stuff. None of it was anything she'd ever seen before, and she was certain that her parents had never opened the cupboards either.

There were likely hundreds of items that she needed to sort through. Luckily, she had the time.

It looked like a wall of junk in front of her. At first glance, she couldn't help but notice that there seemed to be no treasure in sight.

She sighed.

"What have you gotten yourself into?" she whispered to herself.

She knew it would be a massive task, but she was grateful for the distraction. And Charles was still outside, watching over her. So, she felt safe, well-rested, and ready for some cathartic decluttering.

She reached in, grabbed hold of an old box, and wrestled it gently from its resting place. She pulled lightly at it to get it out as smoothly as possible. When the box was free, there was a brief moment of silence, followed by a loud crash as half the contents of the cupboards came crashing down around her.

Chapter Sixteen

Avery let out a loud groan as she assessed the chaos around her. Without really thinking, she sat down and reached for the item nearest to her, tossing it in the trash bag. And she continued that motion for hours. Some items were put on a pile for charity, and before she knew it, she had three whole boxes filled with stuff.

Exhausted and needing a break, Avery decided this was the perfect time to dig into the stew that had been cooking for hours. The smell had filled the house, and Avery realized that she now had an appetite. She ladled a generous portion of stew into a bowl, grabbed some crusty French bread, and poured herself a glass of merlot. Dinner was exactly what Avery needed right now—the stew was comforting, and she was ready to get back to tackling the mess from the cupboard. Avery was pleased by the progress she'd made but knew she still had a lot of work ahead of her.

When the chaos on the ground was sorted, she continued going through the items still left behind in the cupboard. Every few hours, Charles would come in to collect trash bags and boxes and carry them out of the house.

It was the early hours of the morning when she finally made it to the last small pile of items in the cupboard. A small cardboard box was tucked away in the corner. She reached for it and opened it, not giving it much thought.

It was nothing much, just a box filled with old note-books. She was about to empty it into a trash bag when she saw a label on one of them.

G.R.Grier

She stopped dead in her tracks. She knew right away that they were his personal notebooks. She wasn't sure why, but she felt a huge amount of curiosity about them. Imme-diately, she abandoned her decluttering and made herself comfortable on the couch, another glass of merlot in hand. Then, she opened the first book and read the first entry.

Something strange has happened. I have met a woman that has interested me. It is not anything I have ever expected, and I've been perfectly happy on my own until now. What's worse is that she seems interested in me too.

I've arranged to meet her for coffee next week. Perhaps I will cancel. We shall see.

It certainly seemed like it was written by Mr. Grier. As far as Avery knew, he was a lonely man and preferred to stay that way. Yet, there was something about the way he wrote that seemed almost friendly to her, which was not how everyone had described him to be.

She felt that by reading through his personal diaries she was getting to see a side to him that nobody else knew. And she couldn't get enough of it. It seemed strange, after every-thing she'd been through, that she'd be so interested in his life. But she had nothing better to do, and this would be enough to keep her occupied for the next few hours. So she flipped forward and found the entry about his coffee date.

Helena and I met for coffee today. She looked better than when I'd met her. I think perhaps she dressed up for me. I wish I had done the same. I must have looked like an idiot. I had a lovely time, and I find my mind consumed with thoughts of her.

We will meet again next week for some wine.

She read page after page, following his budding relationship with Helena. In his diaries, he wrote about their entire relationship as it developed. She couldn't help but smile at the thought of such a grumpy, anti-social man finding such a sweet and innocent love.

Mr. Grier had fallen head over heels for Helena, and it seemed that she had felt the same way for him. The relationship had quickly become serious, and she was all he wrote about in his diary entries. He would write about the gifts he bought her and the trips that they'd take together. The two of them had really lived a full life. After a while, Helena had moved in with him on the farm, and then the writing stopped.

So, she reached for the next notebook and was excited to see that there was another entry.

Helena and I are to be married next month. Although I had to ask her five times, I have finally won her over. Our relationship is the best thing that has happened to me, and I look forward to growing old together. I do worry about her health. She's developed something that I've never heard of before. The doctors call it agoraphobia. She's suddenly become afraid of the outside world. I don't blame her. It can be cruel.

Slotted into the pages by that entry was a photograph of Helena on their wedding day. She was beautiful. Long blonde hair cascaded over her shoulders as she wore a bright smile. She looked truly happy as she posed outside the courthouse in a chic white mini-dress.

Avery paused her reading and placed the book down on her lap. Why had nobody mentioned that he'd had a wife? She'd spoken to the police and to her family about him. He'd been part of her grandmother's family. How had nobody thought to mention his wife? Where was she when he disappeared? So many questions filled her mind, questions that she knew the diary would answer. So she continued reading, and she learned that they had spent many happy years together. His entries were few and far between after their wedding, but when he wrote, he only wrote about her.

It seemed like a sweet relationship. Helena had done plenty of work on the farm, and soon Avery's questions had been answered. Mr. Grier had been so content with his wife and so unhappy with his family that they'd simply lived a quiet and secretive life on the farm. Nobody had ever learned of his marriage.

He'd felt that he'd never quite fit in with his family, and so they hadn't deserved to know what was happening in his life. She could understand why he might have felt that way, judging by the way everybody had spoken about him. He didn't seem to be popular with anyone but his wife.

But the further she read, the less pretty the picture became. Soon, the isolation and quiet lifestyle had been getting to Helena. The vineyard had started to go downhill, and they were losing money quickly.

I don't know what to do. I feel a lot of pressure from my darling Helena. I want to provide for her, but the truth is I do not know what I am doing. I have nobody to speak to either. I've written off my family. Her ever-growing fear of the outdoors makes things difficult.

Whatever I need to do, I better figure it out quickly. I suspect Helena is losing patience with me.

For a moment, Avery felt sorry for Mr. Grier. Had he felt so rejected by everybody that he felt he had nobody to turn to in his time of need? She wondered if that was why he had run away. She figured that perhaps Helena had left him, and he'd simply left his old life behind, just like she did after James died.

She carried on reading, though, and learned that his concerns had quickly changed into something else entirely. As she read, she found that he became angrier at his wife. He couldn't handle the pressure of being married, keeping his wife happy, and keeping the vineyard alive.

As she read, she came across entries that sounded more and more erratic as time passed. She could no longer put the diaries down at all. She kept reading for hours, eager to learn about what had happened next in the man's life. Then one diary entry stopped her in her tracks.

Things with Helena have reached a tipping point. She has made me a miserable man. I am not welcome in the town and not happy at home. I wish I had never met the woman. She has taken everything from me, even my will to live. She will not leave me, and I cannot leave her. If I do, I risk losing everything. She

*will take my home, my vineyard, and what little
reason I have left to carry on.*

*There is only one way out of this. I hope I can be
forgiven for it.*

Avery's blood ran cold as she read the words. It was clear
that the entry was written by a much older Mr. Grier. The
handwriting was slightly slanted, as often happens when
people start to lose their vision. He certainly seemed
unhinged.

It was the last diary entry, in the last diary. There was no
more left to read. Avery put the book down on the coffee
table, swallowed the last sip of her wine, and thought it all
over. Everything about Mr. Grier had been unexpected
to her.

He'd lived a long, married life that nobody even knew
about. She didn't know what to make of it all. When she
glanced at the book again, something specific caught her eye.
There was something familiar about the way he slanted his
letters.

Avery jumped up and ran towards her handbag,
reaching for the torn-up bits of the first threatening letter
she'd received. When she slumped back on the couch, she
held the pieces up against the book.

A lump formed in her throat as she compared the handwriting. She could feel her palms getting clammy as her
temperature started to climb and a dull headache formed in
the back of her head.

It was a perfect match.

She tossed the notebook aside, wanting it as far away
from her as possible. But as she did so, a small piece of paper
fell out of the back. It was one last entry from Mr. Grier.

Chapter Seventeen

Avery wasn't sure how long she'd have to sit and wait. But she knew he would eventually come. So she sat patiently, sipping at her wine. After all, she had nothing better to do. The vineyard business had been quiet while the investigation was still ongoing. She had decluttered every last shelf and corner of the house to keep herself busy and had finished every book on her list of books to read.

The women of the Stammtisch had come and gone from time to time. But, understandably, they weren't all that comfortable staying there for very long. They would visit, and then all of them would head home before nightfall.

Avery wouldn't leave the house, though. She was expecting someone and wouldn't miss that person for the world. She was almost ready to call it a night and head to bed when she heard a rattling at the back door.

It was the distinct sound of a screwdriver being wedged into the lock. Avery took a deep breath and steeled herself. Then, she turned her chair to face the door and smiled. It wasn't long before the intruder had opened the lock, and the door swung open. Only, he wasn't expecting to see her waiting there for him.

"Good evening, Mr. Grier," Avery greeted him.

A tall old man filled the doorway as he adjusted the hat on his head. In his right hand, he comfortably held a baseball bat.

"I was wondering when you'd show up," she continued, taking a relaxed sip of his wine.

"So you were expecting me?" the old man grumbled.

From where she sat she could smell the whiskey on his breath. It was as if it permeated from his skin, and she could see that he was swaying slightly. She was certain it was his liquid courage for whatever it was he had come to her house to do. She smiled at him.

"I was, indeed, although I didn't think it would take you this long."

The man grunted and shuffled his feet a little, trying to stabilize himself on his wobbly legs. He seemed upset that he had found her so easily. He dropped the screwdriver to the ground with a clang, and it rolled until it came to a neat halt right at Avery's feet.

"How did you know it was me?" he snapped. "Nobody's been able to find me for years, and I've been right under everyone's noses!"

Avery reached over and grabbed the small piece of paper that had fallen out of the back of his notebook. She cleared her throat and read it out loud to him.

I have done something awful. I simply could not take it anymore. My darling Helena left me no choice. I couldn't carry on living that way. But I hadn't considered the psychological consequences. Everywhere I turn, I see her as if her memory is taunting me.

*I must get away. I must go somewhere where there is
no reminder of her. I hope I can find forgiveness.*

"Where'd you find that?" he barked. "That's mine!"

"Then you should have taken a bit more time to pack," Avery shot back, pointing toward the stack of diaries that were piled on the nearby kitchen counter. "I was able to match your handwriting. I know you're the one who's been sending me threats."

The old man sighed and clenched the handle of the bat. But then he started laughing and shaking his head.

"You haven't handed them into the police yet," he chortled. "So I guess I haven't lost yet. I could leave here tonight with all that evidence. I've disappeared once, and I'll do it again. What did you think? We'd have a little chat, and I'd turn myself in? I'm an old man, and I have no intention of going to prison."

Avery eyed the man up and down. Despite being of advanced age, he seemed fit as a fiddle. He looked exactly as everyone had described him. Grumpy and unsmiling. The more she looked at him, the angrier she got. Everything she had been through had been because of him. He had caused her so much stress and trauma, and she hated him for it.

"You didn't have to do what you did, you know," she said bitterly. "There are other ways to end a relationship."

"You didn't know her," he argued. "She was evil that woman was. She sucked the happiness out of me. I couldn't leave her; she would have taken everything from me."

"We both know that's not true," Avery responded. "You just didn't want to put in the work that was necessary."

She was angry at him for what he had done to Helena and for what he had done to her. Nobody deserved to die at the hands of a lazy husband. Not when all they wanted was a better life. He should have simply left her and let her live her life how she wanted to.

He was a selfish, narrow-minded man, and Avery couldn't stand the sight of him.

"You don't know what you're talking about," Mr. Grier said slowly. "I don't see a ring on your finger, so I don't suspect you'd understand."

His comment made her sick. They were nothing alike. She would have done anything to have her husband back, whereas Mr. Grier would have done anything to have his wife removed from his life.

"What did you do to her?" Avery asked, standing up from her chair. "Did you just get tired of her one day and decide that her life needed to end? Was that it?"

Avery could feel her temper rising as her hands shook with anger. But Mr. Grier remained cool as a cucumber.

"She presented me with papers one morning," he said softly. "She was leaving and would take my home and my money, and I would be out on the street. I couldn't exactly let that happen, now could I?"

There was something unsettling and sinister about how casually he spoke about it all. As if it was nothing more than simply popping out to do the groceries.

"So what?" Avery argued. "You could have left and started a new life somewhere else."

"No!" the old man shouted. "This was my life. I invited her to join me and brought her into my home, and she soured it! I couldn't take it anymore!"

Avery knew that Mr. Grier was ready to snap. So she pushed him a little more.

"So what did you do?"

"So I waited until she went to bed, and I smothered her," he said angrily. "I covered her nose and mouth until she stopped breathing, and then I celebrated."

"Why'd you run away then? You got rid of her, and you could have just carried on," Avery asked.

"I thought someone might come looking for her," he said. "I needed to cover my tracks. At first, I thought I could convince everyone that I was dead too. But the useless cops never found that stupid note."

"The note?" Avery asked, trying to piece it all together.

"Yes, the note. The blasted note that you found and took to the police. I'd wanted them to think that I'd been murdered too, but the idiot police never searched the cellars. They took one look at the place and assumed that I'd just disappeared, and that was that."

Mr. Grier clenched his jaw and narrowed his eyes. "Thankfully, nobody came looking for me. I would have gotten away with it if you hadn't been so damn nosy."

Avery slumped down in her chair and smiled at him. That was all that she needed.

"You're a monster," she said quietly. "You signed it with a false initial to send the case in the wrong direction."

Mr. Grier clutched the baseball bat with both hands and took a step inside.

"You have no idea what kind of monster I can be," he growled.

As he lunged toward her, two officers stepped out from the corners of the room and restrained him.

"Mr. Grier, you are under arrest for the murder of Helena Grier!"

Avery watched with joy as they read Mr. Grier his rights, hauling him away to the police van that was parked around the back of the house. Her plan had gone smoothly. When the van door closed on Mr. Grier, she felt the weight of the world lift off her shoulders.

"That was some fine work," Charles said as he approached her.

"I couldn't have done it without your help," Avery said with a smile.

Police officers bagged the diaries and notes, took a statement from Avery and Charles, and left.

"Are you sure you're going to be okay here on your own?" Charles asked as he packed the last of his things in his car.

"Yes," Avery answered. "You've been here for days. Head home and get some rest. I need you back at work on Monday morning."

"Yes, boss," Charles teased, and she watched as he drove off, his headlights disappearing into the distance.

Relieved, Avery finally felt all the exhaustion of the last couple of weeks sneaking up on her. She locked her front door, climbed into bed, turned out the lights, and slept deeply without a single dream.

Avery smiled as she looked out at the sea of smiling faces before her. The garden was filled with tents, drinks, and catering as a live band played smooth jazz in the background. Months of work had gone into that party, and she couldn't believe that the day had finally arrived.

She tapped her knife against her glass, and everybody paused to face her with Sprinkles seated well-mannered at her side.

"Ladies and gentlemen, could I have just a moment of your time?" she said, smiling brightly. "I'd like to thank every single one of you for coming out today. A special thank you to my mother, father, Tiffany, the women of the Stammtisch, and of course, Charles, who have all been so patient with me on this journey. I am proud to say that the time has finally arrived."

Avery turned to her left and reached for the large gold scissors. She hovered the open blades over the bright red ribbon that stretched out before her.

"I would like to declare Cellar Vie Guest House officially open!"

Avery snipped the ribbon, and it drifted down on either side of her as the garden erupted into applause.

The End.

⁓

If you loved this book, you'll definitely want to check out *Murder at the Festival!*

Visit https://amzn.to/41erfuL to get *Murder at the Festival* now.

Here's a sneak peek...

A small town wine festival. An intriguing stone clutched in the cold grip of a dead tourist. No one expects his death would be ruled a murder.

This full-length whodunit will keep you guessing at every turn. Join Avery, Sprinkles, and the gang from Le Blanc Cellars for another adventure!

Click here to get *Murder at the Festival* now.

Turn the page to start the first chapter!

Murder at the Festival

SNEAK PEEK

Back in her hometown, city girl Avery Parker is finally settling in after her husband's sudden passing.

The town is abuzz with the annual wine festival and Avery is amped to show off Le Blanc Cellars' newest release. But between pours of their famed Chenin Blanc, a lifeless body is found.

A curious gray stone clutched in the cold grip of a dead tourist intrigues the locals, and no one expects his death would be ruled a murder.

Driven by empathy for the dead man's widow, Avery pieces together the puzzle and unearths a scandal larger than she could ever have imagined.

As long as she doesn't get in her own way, Avery might bring justice for a tourist's untimely demise. That is, unless she becomes a victim herself.

With more twists than the vines at Le Blanc Cellars, Murder at the Festival will have readers guessing this whodunit.

Wine pairings and irresistible recipes included!

Visit https://amzn.to/41erfuL to get
Murder at the Festival now.

~

Chapter One

It wasn't often that the park looked as festive as it did during the Winter Wine Festival. Avery hadn't been to the festival in many years, as most winters she'd been in the city. That year Le Blanc Cellars had the opportunity to represent themselves at the festival and Avery was proud to see her vineyard such a success.

It was a big deal, and the few friends she had in town made sure to remind her of it for the weeks leading up to the festival. Not only was it an opportunity for Le Blanc Cellars to get some decent marketing, but Cellar Vie Guest House was booked full for the week of the festival.

For Avery, it meant there was plenty to celebrate. And she was in the right place for a celebration. The first day of the festival had been a success, and the night was bound to be even busier. There was a popular band scheduled to play, and the air was filled with the aroma of all the best street food the city had to offer.

"Remember how we used to walk through this market looking for any fallen coins so we could buy snacks?" Tiffany asked between sips. "It always was, and still is, the event of the year!"

Memories of those days came flooding back to her. It was a time when children could run freely through the festival without any concerns about security. Avery wished she could go back to those days before she knew what stress, grief, anger, or loneliness was. She remembered how carefree she felt as she would run through the fields, her head constantly bent down, searching for anything that seemed too shiny to be grass.

They would get completely hopped up on sugar, then go home and watch musicals until they eventually crashed. Everyone had fun then—Avery, Tiffany, and their parents. The memories were filled with laughter, music, and just the right amount of chaos.

Avery laughed. "I remember it all too well. I must admit, though, the festival is a lot more fun now that I'm old enough to drink the wine."

Avery was doing her best to take part in the conversation, but she was distracted by the beauty of the festival. It had come a long way since she'd last attended. She remembered it to be a couple of wine farms offering tastings and maybe the local karaoke bar would set up a temporary gig.

What Avery saw that night was vastly different. Strings with small lights wrapped through the air created a soft glow that could be seen from blocks away. Soft jazz filtered through the park, always at the same volume no matter where she walked.

The food was good, the atmosphere was refreshing, and she felt proud of something for the first time in a long time. She had put months of work into designing the Le Blanc Cellars stall. Everything about the wines, display, and wine-tasting experience had been perfected. And it seemed to be paying off.

To a certain extent, Avery had nothing to worry about. Her businesses were doing well, she had made friends, and she was healing from the death of her husband one day at a time. It was never going to be easy, but Avery had enough to keep her occupied.

She was about to say something to Tiffany when a stumbling man knocked the wine right out of her hand. Red wine spilled all over her and a nearby passerby. In fact, he had hit her hard enough that if Tiffany hadn't caught her, Avery would have fallen down too.

"She did it!" he yelled as he fell. "She's the one you're looking for!"

Avery stared at the man. He was a short, chubby man with pink cheeks and small round glasses. There was little about him that was attractive. He hit the ground with a loud thud, and a moment later, a small crowd gathered to help him up.

"What was that about?" Avery laughed as she inspected the wine stains on her shirt. "That, my dear, is the look of someone who has tasted far too much of what our vineyards have to offer," Tiffany replied.

When Avery glanced back, the man had been seated on a bench and left there to sober up. Tiffany and Avery headed to the ladies room in an attempt to clean out the wine stains that decorated Avery's shirt.

"Shall we wash it out with white wine?" Tiffany joked.

It was a good joke, good enough to have Avery laughing out loud. Her laughs echoed off the bathroom walls.

"Maybe if I just cover it with more wine, it will look like I dressed up for the occasion?" Avery suggested through giggles.

"Worth a try," Tiffany said.

"No, you can't be serious," Avery responded. She had been joking, but something in Tiffany's eyes said that she didn't think it was all that much of a joke. Tiffany led her back out onto the lawn, just behind the bathrooms.

Then Tiffany motioned for Avery to wait for her while she disappeared into the crowd, returning with two glasses of red wine.

"Now, hold still," Tiffany commanded.

Realizing that she really had nothing to lose and the blouse was already ruined, she nodded, giving Tiffany the go-ahead. Avery did her best to stand still between bouts of laughter as Tiffany threw two glasses of wine at her. The wine splashed, causing a huge mess on the ground at Avery's feet, but tipsiness had done a great job of dulling her embarrassment.

"That actually looks better!" Tiffany cheered.

"Except for the smell," Avery said as she blushed. "I smell like the bottom of a barrel."

"It's a wine festival," Tiffany whispered, linking her arm to Avery's. "Nobody will notice. Everything here smells like red wine."

"Isn't the mayor coming today?" Avery asked. "I heard some visitors saying something along those lines, and I thought I saw him earlier, but it was very brief."

Tiffany shrugged. "He usually comes on the first day of the festival, but I've been here all day and I haven't seen him yet. Maybe he'll come tomorrow."

"That's strange," Avery replied. "I was certain I had seen him. Maybe he only stayed for a bit."

"It's really great to see you having some fun," Tiffany said with a smile as she nudged Avery in the ribs. "Things have been hard on you. I'm happy you're able to let loose a little."

"Well, as of right now, I've decided to make it a habit to have fun," Avery joked, as she fixed her shirt.

It was the most fun that Avery had experienced in ages. They were lucky enough to make it in time to get a spot on the lawn and watch the band perform. To Avery's surprise, she knew the words to every song they played and sang along loudly with the rest of the crowd.

For a brief moment, she felt like a teenager again. The atmosphere was the same, and everyone around her was having a good time too. With the lights that ran through the park, the smell of food cooking over a fire, and live music, she felt like nothing could possibly go wrong.

It had been a long time since Avery had allowed herself to let loose like that. She realized that perhaps she had been taking life far too seriously, and made a tipsy reminder to herself to enjoy life a little more. She wanted countless nights like the one she was having, and she felt determined to make it happen.

~

"Don't you have to clean up your stall?" Tiffany asked as they made their way to the parking lot.

The band had finished, and the crowd was leaving the park. Avery had always been amazed at how quickly a busy place can become completely empty. Soon, there would be nobody, and the lights would be turned off. The park would rest until the next morning when the second day of the festival would commence.

"Nah," Avery said, stepping carefully over the cables that led from behind the stage. "I've hired some young folk to do that for me. Best decision I've made so far," she joked.

Avery and Tiffany used each other for support to make sure they'd walk upright and neither of them would trip over anything in the dark. It was a habit they had formed after one too many bruises during their college years.

"Do you remember that time we tumbled down that hill after the art exhibition?" Tiffany laughed. "I bruised every single one of my fingers and eight of my toes."

"I remember!" Avery cackled. "That was tough to explain to your parents too. What a weird injury!"

"I have to admit, though, I can feel the age in my bones. I'm eager to get into bed," Tiffany confessed.

"Yes, please," Avery agreed. "I'd like to go home, too. I'm sure Sprinkles is worried sick about me."

Something about the last statement made Tiffany laugh so hard that tears were rolling down her face. Avery didn't really understand what was so funny, but then again, that was normal in their friendship. Before they made it back to the edge of the park, they noticed a large crowd had formed.

"What's going on there?" Avery asked, tugging on Tiffany's arm. "Let's go see."

They wormed their way through the crowd, and Avery couldn't help but notice that many of the faces she passed were pale and concerned. That's when she saw the police tape. It was the drunkard from before.

His limp body sat exactly where he had been left when he'd been helped off the ground hours before. There were murmurs traveling fast through the crowd as police did their best to do their job, ignoring the questions of the spectators.

The man's wife was screaming on the sidelines, reaching for her dead husband through loud wails. For a brief moment, the woman tried to fight one of the police officers before collapsing to the ground and sobbing loudly into her hands.

"How terrible," Tiffany whispered.

One of the officers gently lifted her from the ground and ushered her away from the bench. That's when Avery understood precisely what was going on. She recognized the woman's behavior. She'd been there herself not too long ago.

The man was clearly dead. He had hardly moved since he had been placed there. The police tried desperately to usher the crowd away, and Avery took one last glance before respecting their request and walking away.

As she looked at the man, she realized he was tightly grasping a stone in his hand. She could just make out the word *Heron* painted on it in what looked like red lipstick. It seemed like a bizarre thing to reach for in his final moments.

But she had seen him when he fell, and she thought that she would have remembered him clutching onto something so odd.

"Do you think it's possible to drink yourself to death like that?" she asked, suddenly concerned for her own health and safety. "If so, then I need to start taking things easy."

Tiffany scoffed. "Not at a festival like this one, surely. Although, if you ask me, death by wine tasting doesn't sound like a bad way to go. Maybe he bumped his head when he fell?"

"How hard can you bump your head against a soft lawn?" Avery asked, frowning as she thought it all over.

The women walked in silence for a moment before Tiffany shrugged. "Maybe he just had a heart attack or something."

Avery thought it over for a moment, and then decided that a heart attack was her favorite explanation for it. It still didn't really make sense, given the man's behavior before he fell and the fact that a wine festival hardly seemed like the place to have a heart attack. Then again, Avery was no medical professional, and she couldn't think of anything else that made sense, either.

Everybody around them seemed to be discussing it, talking about the dead man and giving their own explanations for what had happened. By the time they reached the car, there were hundreds of theories traveling through the town gossip.

"A death at the wine festival," Tiffany said quietly. "Talk about a buzz kill."

It was a good joke, but Avery had a hard time laughing at it. Tiffany always had the worst timing when it came to humor. She didn't often tell jokes, but when she did, there was a strong chance that the timing was completely inappropriate.

The women hopped into a cab and headed home. The cab driver had already heard the news about the dead body. One of his friends who had attended the festival had phoned him to tell him about it. The gossip really was traveling fast.

Avery groaned. She knew that it meant the following day would be a tough one. She'd likely have to answer the same questions over again, considering that there wasn't often anything new to talk about. She didn't like getting involved with town gossip, but she needed to make some sales. She was running the vineyard, so she needed to make sure that anybody interested in their wines knew she was equally as interested in them. So, she didn't have a choice.

Visit https://amzn.to/41erfuL to get
Murder at the Festival now.

Recipes

No wonder it's one of Avery's favorite breakfasts!

Souffle Toast (serves 8)

1 loaf soft French bread (sliced diagonally, 1½"
thick)
1 quart heavy whipping cream
10 eggs
¾ cup orange juice
½ cup sugar
1 pinch salt
1 teaspoon ground cinnamon
2 tablespoons vanilla extract
butter for frying
powdered sugar for dusting
strawberries, blueberries, blackberries

- Mix whipping cream, eggs, juice, sugar, salt,
  vanilla, and cinnamon until well combined.
- Pour over bread slices.

- Cover with plastic wrap and refrigerate for one hour.
- Remove bread and dump liquid.
- Preheat oven to 450 degrees.
- Melt a pat of butter on a pan over medium heat.
- Cook bread until golden brown.
- Place bread in baking pan and bake at 450 degrees for 5-7 minutes.
- Bread will puff up like a soufflé.
- Top with berries and dust generously with powdered sugar.
- Serve immediately with maple syrup and sausage or bacon.
- Enjoy!

Pair with cinnamon latte and/or mimosas

Cinnamon Latte (serves 4)

2 cups strong coffee
1 teaspoon ground cinnamon
2 tablespoons sugar
5 cups 2% milk

- Mix cinnamon and sugar with a cup of milk in medium pot.
- Add remaining milk to the pot and bring to a boil.
- Turn off heat as soon as the mixture comes to a boil.
- Split hot coffee among 4 coffee mugs.
- Add milk mixture to coffee mugs.
- Garnish with whipped cream and a stick of cinnamon if you're feeling fancy!

Mimosa (serves 4)

8 ounces juice (orange, pineapple, mango, or pome-granate)
8 ounces sparkling wine

- Pour juice equally into chilled champagne flutes.
- Top with sparkling wine.

A perfect lunch with girlfriends!

Couscous with Pan-Fried Shrimp and Asparagus (serves 4)

5 tablespoons olive oil, divided
2 tablespoons lemon juice
2 tablespoons shallots, minced
1 tablespoon fresh dill, chopped
1½ teaspoon Dijon mustard
½ teaspoon Kosher salt, divided
freshly ground black pepper
1 cup Israeli/pearl couscous
2¼ cups chicken broth
1 pound uncooked peeled and deveined medium shrimp
1 bunch asparagus, tough stems removed and cut into 2" slices

- In a large bowl, prepare dressing. Whisk 2 tablespoons of olive oil, lemon juice, shallot, dill, mustard, ¼ teaspoon of the salt, and a few grinds of black pepper together. Set aside.
- In a large saucepan over medium heat, add 1 tablespoon oil. Warm through until shimmery in pan.
- Add couscous and cook until light brown and toasty (don't forget to stir!) for about 3 minutes.
- Add broth slowly and stir in ¼ teaspoon salt.
- Bring mixture to a boil.
- Reduce heat to medium-low. Simmer uncovered for about 10 minutes total (until couscous is tender).

- Meanwhile, in a separate pan, warm 1 tablespoon of oil on medium-high heat. When oil is shimmery, add asparagus and sauté for about 2 minutes.
- Add remaining tablespoon of oil to pan. Stir in shrimp and cook for 3 minutes. Season with salt and pepper.
- Drain couscous. Add couscous and asparagus/shrimp mixture to dressing. Toss to combine.

Pair with chilled pinot gris or rosé

Comfort food at its best

Braised Beef with Mushrooms (serves 8)

5 lbs chuck roast, cut into 4" pieces, fat removed
2 tablespoons olive oil
1 tablespoon kosher salt
1 medium sized onion, diced
2 large carrots, peeled and diced
2 bay leaves
4 garlic cloves, crushed
2 tablespoons tomato paste
3 tablespoons flour
3 cups light red wine
1 lb cremini mushrooms, cut in half
3 sprigs of fresh thyme
pepper

- Preheat oven to 350°F.
- Pat meat dry with paper towel.
- Generously salt and pepper meat all over.
- In Dutch oven (or heavy pot), heat oil until shimmering.
- Brown all sides of the meat (2 minutes per side). Set aside.
- Reduce heat to medium-low. Add onions, carrots, and bay leaves.
- Sauté carrots and onions until just tender (5 minutes).
- Add garlic and cook 2 more minutes.
- Stir in tomato paste. Sprinkle mixture with flour.
- Stir in the wine slowly while adding mushrooms.

- Arrange meat in pot in single layer.
- Add thyme to pot and bring to a boil.
- Cover pot and put in oven.
- Cook for 3 hours.
- Serve with mashed potatoes.

Pair with cabernet sauvignon or merlot